SISTER AGNES

THE WORLD'S OLDEST SERIAL KILLER

BY

Domhnall O'Donoghue

Published by Agatha Publishing
ISBN 978-1-3999-2267-8

A CIP catalogue record for this book is
available from the British Library.

Second Edition 2022
Originally Published by
Tirgearr Publishing
in 2016

DEDICATION

For those who believe that life has no Best Before

PROLOGUE

THE MEATH CHRONICLE, 06 FEBRUARY 1898

There was cause for celebration in the village of Kilberry this week. Yesterday, cigars were passed around following the arrival of bonnie baby Butsy Miller. While her proud parents, farmers Seán and Máire, were not available to speak to *The Meath Chronicle*—likely too busy fawning over the latest member of their family—a loose-lipped neighbour explained that it was a hectic day on the Miller's farm. He revealed that the couple's bundle of joy arrived seconds after one of their prized cows had also given birth.

'One weighed a fine eight pounds,' the knowledgeable neighbour explained, 'while the scales showed the other to be a mighty eighty!'

For the sake of Mrs Miller, we only hope the poor woman delivered the lighter of the two.

'With all these happy and healthy additions,' the neighbour added, a mischievous glint in his eye, 'I'd wager the Millers are over the moo-n!'

Indeed. Additionally, if this jokester's memory is trustworthy, the infant will be pleased to learn that she comes from an almost imperishable clan. Rather impressively, her two great-grandmothers did not relinquish life until they had both passed the century mark.

To that end, we trust little Butsy has the sense to squirrel away as many hours of sleep as possible—while she can—for it appears to be written that a long and venturesome road lies ahead of the youngster.

ONE

For as long as anyone could remember, Sister Agatha wore tinted glasses —a stylish accessory that added definition to her soft, bulbous face. She wasn't sensitive to the sun; in fact, the nun often enjoyed lolling about the convent's gardens on a summer's day. No, the real reason she armed herself with shaded eyewear was to convince people that she was listening to them when, in reality, she was doing like Rip Van Winkle and catching forty winks. Having graced God's earth for one hundred and eighteen years, she had, understandably, tired of having to indulge people and their embarrassment of mundane predicaments.

Of course, Sister Agatha knew that she was professionally obliged to provide a sympathetic ear to her parishioners, but, some days, the old doll hadn't the interest. Such as this morning. As she sat in the waiting room of the doctor's surgery, located on Navan's busy Abbey Road, Sister Agatha thanked the good Lord above that she had come equipped with her invaluable tinted glasses. Doreen Cooney, the town bore, had made a beeline for the nun when she spotted her on arrival. Despite claiming to be in the throes of a brutal battle with tonsillitis, the gabby school principal was in full voice, waxing lyrical about her adorable new cat, Lolita, and the crazy escapades they got up to together. (It was little wonder Mr Cooney had recently accepted a job on the oil rigs off the coast of Scotland; the constant drilling was sure to be a welcome reprieve from his wife's relentless chatter.)

'Sister, I could honestly spend the whole day long squeezing and tickling and kissing Lolita!' Doreen now readily confessed. 'You should hear the adorable sounds the little cutey pie makes when she's indigest-'

2

Before Doreen could complete the sentence, Sister Agatha hightailed it to the land of Nod—and thanks to her extremely helpful spectacles, nobody knew any better. And this is where she remained until the rugged Doctor McManus emerged from his surgery some ten minutes later.

'My appointment book tells me that it's time to give me star patient her monthly once-over,' he announced from his door, resisting the urge to give the proud and self-sufficient super-centenarian a helping hand.

Sister Agatha shook off her slumber and bade Mrs Cooney goodbye (while secretly thanking her for the rather lovely catnap).

'I was just about to show you some of our homemade videos,' Doreen lamented. 'I suppose I could wait until you're finished?'

Sister Agatha pretended not to hear this horrid suggestion and quickly shut the surgery door behind her. Every first Wednesday of the month, the formidable nun sashayed into this medical centre for a straightforward, on-the-off-chance examination. Every time, Doctor McManus would probe her from head to toe, then praise her extraordinary genes to the high heavens—a place the one-hundred-and-eighteen-year-old had no interest in frequenting anytime soon. Sister Agatha felt confident today would be no different.

* * *

Sister Agatha had been the proud owner of an entirely different name before becoming a Bride of Christ. Born in early February 1898—the same year C.S. Lewis and George Gershwin also took their first breaths—Butsy Miller was the most adorable baby in the whole county of Meath, thanks to her head of precious curls.

Her parents were farmers in Kilberry, a simple village located a country mile north of Navan. Since their wedding night, the couple had tried desperately for a child, but as they approached their mid-forties, it seemed the good Lord had other ideas for them. However, the seeds of Butsy Miller were miraculously sown just as Mr Miller was about to throw in the towel. (Quite literally—Mrs Miller passionately believed that cleanliness was next to godliness, so insisted that her poor husband washed thoroughly before every attempt to generate offspring. She rightly argued that farming was a hard slog that didn't promote pleasant bodily odours.)

Nine months later, during the first week of spring, Kilberry saw the rain fall, but its population rise—from two hundred and four to two hundred and five. Neighbours and relatives gathered around, who had high hopes for the community's youngest member.

'What a charming wife she will make someday—look at her beauty!'

'What first-class curls!'

'Notice how large and sturdy her hands are—she is sure to follow in her parents' footsteps and become a farmer one day!'

The initial excitement petered out when the busy stork brought Philomena O'Rourke a set of twins a week later, stealing Butsy's thunder and sending Kilberry's population skyrocketing to a hefty two hundred and seven. Mr and Mrs Miller were thankful for the distraction because they now had their little cherub all to themselves. They had no idea who she might marry or what she might become in the future; for now, they just wanted to enjoy their daughter's company.

And how they marvelled at the fact that thanks to her colourful, chubby cheeks combined with the rebellious curl that always stood ramrod straight no matter how much they tinkered with it, their little Butsy Miller bore an uncanny resemblance to a Hallowe'en pumpkin.

* * *

Perched on top of a plinth inside Doctor McManus' examination room, Sister Agatha's veil was now removed, revealing a shock of white, curly hair. Her habit was also cast aside; the delicate, ivory slip that she wore perfectly showcased her sinewy arms— the sight of which would probably have left most people half her age green with envy. Completely under Doctor McManus' spell, Sister Agatha was, as always, identical to an obedient schoolgirl, doing everything the dashing medic demanded of her with added enthusiasm.

'Would me favourite patient mind sticking out her tongue for me?'

His favourite patient most certainly would not mind; in fact, Sister Agatha outstretched it so far that a light aircraft could have landed on it.

'Excellent,' he gushed, tickled by her spirit. 'And now, could you say "Awww" for me, Sister?'

Upon hearing this command, the nun imagined she was on the Sydney Opera House stage and belted out an aria—almost deafening the poor man in the process.

'Sounds good to me!' he noted while also hoping that the ringing in his ears would soon subside.

'One last thing, and then I'll send you on your merry way, Sister. Could you *gently* breathe into this stethoscope?'

Having little interest in doing anything in moderation, the venerable dame inhaled so much oxygen into her lungs, Doctor McManus worried they would suffer the same fate as the Hindenburg airship. Sister Agatha was as fit as the proverbial fiddle, and each month, she desperately wanted to remind the doctor of that very fact.

It wasn't just Sister Agatha who was a creature of habit. Without fail, at the end of each examination, Doctor McManus would playfully pinch her rosy cheeks and say in his gloriously thick Navan accent: 'Ye couldn't knock a bother outta ye, Sister!' And, just like a lovesick teenager, she would laugh coquettishly, swat his hand away, and make some comment of the garden variety, like: 'Still time to run the marathon, do you think, Doctor?' or 'The perfect girl to take home to your mother, so?'

Today, he failed to utter his well-rehearsed line about being unable to knock a bother out of her. That wasn't the only change to the script. Doctor McManus, ever the gentleman, would typically assist his star pupil onto the floor, help her dress, then lead her to the seat in front of his desk, where he would praise her to the hilt. But this morning, for some reason, he also ignored this age-old custom and, instead, excused himself, promising to return in a few minutes as he had to 'double-check something'.

'Don't worry, Sister, I'll send in a nurse to help put you back together!' he quipped, but Sister Agatha did not laugh at his joke this time. She felt a knot in her stomach, convinced that the good doctor had discovered something untoward, and the prognosis was not favourable. Had he popped out for a drop of brandy to work up the courage to tell her the jig was up? Maybe he was trying to convince a colleague to do his dirty work for him? Or had he taken to the hills like the fearful Sister Mary Bernadette once did after she had accidentally left a bath running, resulting in part of the convent's second floor caving in—and almost killing Sister Zina in the process?

Some unfamiliar nurse now sauntered in, briefly preventing the nun from indulging in her morbidity. Judging by the lack of grace with which the young woman assisted the hundred-and-eighteen-year-old back into her habit, Sister Agatha wagered that ballet was not something she had ever practised. Speaking of habits, most people insisted on shouting at the elderly nun despite her exemplary hearing.

'Lift your arms for me, will ye, Sister? Your arms – ARMS!'

Instead of taking the nurse to task for her abrupt manner, Sister Agatha thought the quickest way to end this disagreeable encounter was to hold her whisht and comply with orders. 'Silence is golden' was Sister Agatha's mantra, which had stood her in good stead over the years. (Her first Mother Superior had the temper of a Spanish bull, so both she and her cohorts at the convent implemented that maxim time and time again.)

Job finally completed, the patient sat alone again, unsure of what she should do next. Her stomach grumbled – a reminder that it was fast approaching lunchtime. While she never overlooked a good feeding—especially when Sister Josephine's delicious tomato, lentil and orange soup appeared on the menu—she wasn't sure if she could handle any food, such was her anxiety.

Something is amiss, I know it!

Unable to stand the suspense any longer, she marched over to the door, took a deep breath and swung it open—an action she immediately regretted doing. Doctor Manus stood beside a colleague, but they were not chatting about the latest sporting event as she had secretly hoped. Instead, the pair discussed something much more gruesome than anything a spectator might witness at a boxing match or rugby game: Sister Agatha's imminent demise.

'Ye could give her a week, but I think it's best to put her out of her misery straight away.'

'I think you're right, James,' his colleague added, solemnly nodding his head.

Sister Agatha stood aghast. Not only was she being told that it was curtains, but to add insult to injury, her seemingly ambrosial Doctor McManus intended to send her to the slaughterhouse right there and then!

If I had Sister Josephine's hot tomato soup in my hand, I'd drown the barbarian in it!

Sister Agatha thought it best to skip Godspeeds and cheerios and disappeared out the exit.

No wonder that young nurse was in such foul form, Sister Agatha thought, emerging into the car park—*who wouldn't be, working under such a duplicitous brute of a man as Doctor McManus.*

* * *

Four-legged Lolita had experienced a tumultuous start in life. Her original owner, an English professor at Trinity College, had become pregnant and suddenly developed a strong reaction to cat hair. While heart-breaking, Professor Poulter was forced to send the ginger feline packing. The second home that Lolita had ended up in was owned by an elderly, eccentric Chinese lady who had few friends due to her dramatic tendencies. Just as Lolita was happily settling into her new lodgings, a terrifying roar sounded throughout the house. The cat discovered Old Lady Yip holding a framed picture of an elderly man wearing a large conical hat.

'Lolita, Lolita, Lolita!' she repeated, tears cascading down her cheeks.

The batty woman had convinced herself that her new pet was the reincarnation of her late grandfather, and that simply wouldn't do—she had little interest in the violent man when he lived; she had even less now that he was pushing up daisies. And so, Lolita was shown the door once again.

Her third and final dwelling place transpired to be a much

more favourable arrangement—well, initially, at least. Doreen Cooney had become quite lonely since her husband had secured employment on an oil rig close to the Shetland Islands. With her grown-up children having long since fled the nest, Doreen had longed for a bit of company in the evenings, which is when she saw Old Lady Yip's advertisement in the shop window.

Lolita was an extremely playful and affectionate cat, and while most humans found Doreen to be insufferable, animals were not nearly as judgmental—especially if they were fed up with going from pillar to post. They were the perfect partners-in-crime, constantly larking about—so much so, the pair often wished that there were more hours in the day. But this initial happiness proved fleeting, unfortunately.

This morning, Doreen had awoken with a nasty dose of tonsillitis. She made an appointment with the lovely Doctor McManus, leaving Lolita to enjoy a little downtime on her own. Sadly, that adage about curiosity killing the cat had much merit today. When the fluffy Persian explored Doreen's converted garage, she became intrigued by the treadmill that her owner had purchased several years earlier to shift a few pesky Christmas pounds. Unable to resist temptation, Lolita jumped onto it with such enthusiasm that the contraption immediately sprung to life, hurling the poor *creatúr* against the wall with a ferocious bang!

Mrs Monaghan, a neighbour, dashed over to investigate the source of the racket when, through the window, she saw poor Lolita sprawled out on the floor, clinging to dear life. No longer entrusted with the spare keys after she had ransacked Doreen's makeup box when the Cooneys were out of town, Mrs Monaghan called her neighbour with the news. Having worked as a veterinary nurse in her younger days, Mrs Monaghan informed Doreen that Lolita could last the week, but it might be for the best to put her out of her misery right there and then. In the surgery, despite fragile tonsils, Doreen released a roar that would shame a thunderstorm.

'Why do all the things that I love the most leave me?' she demanded to know before fleeing the building.

Doctor McManus, who had been examining Sister Agatha at the time, left his star patient alone to investigate the commotion outside. Having been an animal lover all his life, he was saddened by the revelations. When he discussed the situation with his colleague, he couldn't help but agree with Mrs Monaghan's recommendations.

'Yes, ye could give her a week, but I think it's best to put her out of her misery straight away.'

If only Lolita were more like Sister Agatha, Doctor McManus mused. She was a cat who certainly had nine lives, and if the examination he had just completed suggested anything, it was clear that she probably had another good ten years left in her.

* * *

Paul, Sister Agatha's faithful taxi driver, waited in the medical centre's car park, listening to a trashy talk show on the radio. Being a sucker for good old-fashioned debate, he always looked forward to discussing in detail the various arguments with Sister Agatha following her monthly consultations—often too much detail, she felt. He had even once enjoyed celebrity status in the town after calling one such radio programme. The topic under discussion questioned whether women 'should be more mindful of their age when kitting out their wardrobes'. Most callers had felt that women of a particular vintage should not wear revealing garments such as bikinis or miniskirts.

'It's disgustin'—I don't wanna be lookin' at their wrinkly bits and bobs.'

Having ferried around a gal who predated radio broadcasting itself, Paul, on the other hand, believed that the elderly should be revered and not criticised for their sartorial choices. They should be free to strut about in whatever they fancied – even a couple of fig leaves to protect their modesty. Having seen red, Paul swore black and blue at all the sanctimonious so-and-sos for being rude and mean-spirited.

'Why don't you go and shove your opinions up your dirty fu—'

Beep, beep, beep.

Such was his rage, Paul failed to realise that he had been cut off for over five minutes.

As a direct result of his friendship with Sister Agatha, Paul had long since concluded that age was indeed just a number. If he had a bottom dollar in his possession, the chap would use it to bet that his favourite old-timer was going to outlive everybody and everything—even his immortal cactus plant! He had often told the lads in Bermingham's bar what an honour it was to drive her around and often hypothesised that he would die a happy man should he reach half her age. (Paul was only forty-one but had already suffered two triple by-passes. Sixty cigarettes a day, compounded by little exercise, nightly takeaways and those tipples in his local—came at a high price he was recently discovering.)

Today, Paul didn't get an opportunity to relay his opinions to Sister Agatha about some sleep-deprived plumber who had just revealed live on the radio that he reluctantly shared a bed with his wife due to her chattering teeth. When the nun abruptly jumped into the back seat, she was visibly distressed and not in the slightest bit interested in engaging in any conversation.

'Is everything alright, Sis—'

'Get out of here, Paul. Quick! There's no time for idle chitchat!'

This abruptness also led to Paul forgetting to tell his favourite passenger all about that silly Mrs Cooney's hysterics moments earlier and that it looked as if her new cat hadn't long left for the world. Instead, as ordered, Paul put his foot on the pedal but hoped the gal sitting behind him was all right. If not, who else would give out to him for being unable to show moderation when it came to his nightly libations?

* * *

Forget Navan Carpets, Tara Mines, or the beloved shopping centre—when it came to the Royal County's largest and most affluent town, nothing or nobody was cherished more than its oldest resident, Sister Agatha. Local hydrographer Sir Francis Beaufort invented the scale to measure wind, but the centuries-old apparatus could have been created with Sister Agatha in mind, for she was an incalculable force of nature. Wherever she went—adoration in Saint Mary's Church, cheering on the county football team in Páirc Tailteann, or getting some fresh air into her well-worn lungs in the nearby Dalgan Park—Sister Agatha was always surrounded by a legion of fans. So long as she was kitted out with her tinted glasses and continued to master the knack of being able to doze off while vertical, she was delighted to be the centre of attention. Except when she was enjoying her weekly Cappuccino.

Following her successful examinations on the first Wednesday of every month, Sister Agatha would treat Paul to a cup of coffee and some delicious cake in the Ardboyne Hotel. Those rare moments of indulgence demanded peace and quiet, with nary a sinner being allowed to interrupt. Like every other Irish person, she had been a tea connoisseur all her life, but when the introduction of coffee in their many guises had swept the country in the nineties, rather unashamedly, she jumped horses. While some might have viewed this move as heretical, Sister Agatha had argued that she limited her intake of coffee to Cappuccinos alone, which were, after all, named after the famous band of Italian, brown-robed monks.

'My switch is simply a celebration of my religious vows!' she had often waffled.

Today, the gal was in no mood for such blissful refreshments and demanded to be taken back to the convent post haste. She didn't want to cause Paul any alarm—she was very fond of him, even though an infant could take better care of himself—so decided to keep what she had just heard in the medical centre under her veil. Passing Watergate Street's stone-clad Town Hall before continuing along the Ring Road, Sister Agatha stared forlornly out the car window, where she spied a lone magpie flying over the chirpy Boyne River. There was little need for a bird to tell her that today was a day of sorrow.

They made their way out the Dublin Road towards Johnstown, where the rather austere-looking Order of Saint Aloysius convent had stood for almost three centuries. Sister Agatha's mind was ablaze with questions: was it something she had done—or not done—that had now led her to death's door? She had religiously followed that dictum about your body being your temple, so she was at a loss as to why Doctor McManus claimed she was on the verge of kicking the proverbial bucket. Unlike her driver, cigarettes had never passed her lips while alcohol was a relative stranger to her, so those life-shortening vices could be discounted. Granted, she was no Sonia O'Sullivan, but the nun had made light work out of numerous pairs of runners in her youth, jogging up and down the leafy ramparts most afternoons. And as for those sunny summer days when she and the other sisters had enjoyed endless games of rounders…

What's more, when it came to cooking, Sister Josephine was nothing short of a culinary doyenne, ensuring that the Order of Saint Aloysius' inhabitants always received what was needed to maintain a healthy body. So, Sister Agatha's sudden downfall had nothing to do with being starved of her five-a-day. In terms of her health, she had always ensured that she was in mint condition.

Why am I now being punished?

If it weren't for the fact that she was a God-fearing nun, the same four-lettered word that the convent's gardener had used when a wing of the building had accidentally caught fire would have passed her lips. And even if it had, who could blame her? After all, Doctor McManus had just disclosed that the improbable vow she made many decades earlier had—like the conservatory and storeroom—gone up in smoke.

To be the oldest person in the world.

TWO

It happened almost overnight: one minute, Butsy was rolling around on all fours; the next, she was an intelligent young woman, ready to take on the world. Neither parent had dedicated much of their lives to their education, so they were pleasantly surprised when Butsy excelled in school. A general all-rounder, geography, in particular, was her strong point. She was spellbound by all the countries in the world, in addition to her dear Ireland. She had read and re-read Jules Verne's *Around the World in Eighty Days* and thought it the most fantastic adventure ever told and spent hours wondering if, one day, she would receive an opportunity to visit such exotic places for herself.

'Cowsheds don't clean themselves,' Mr Miller continuously reminded her when he caught her daydreaming about such things.

Those initial suspicions about her future beauty proved accurate, and every time she passed Kilberry village, every head, young and old, would turn. But there was just one person whose attention Butsy craved, and that was Pádraig Keogh—the tall, sophisticated son of her parents' disagreeable landlady. Fortunately, the chap, three years her senior, was equally smitten, if not more so. Whenever he cycled past the Miller's farm, Pádraig would ring his bell and wave frantically at his beautiful and statuesque Venus. Once, endorsing that saying that love was blind, he'd failed to notice a large, broken branch and went head-first over the handlebars, landing plumb in the middle of a thorny ditch.

While Butsy often had her head in the clouds, her feet were firmly rooted in reality. She had enough smarts to realise that any relationship with Pádraig would be a bust. Yes, she may have been a walking encyclopaedia concerning the Great War currently ravaging the world, for example, but she remained a humble farmer's daughter. Pádraig Keogh, on the other hand, was the heir to an estate that could be used to pay a king's ransom.

'The fella who's lucky enough to win your heart will love you, warts and all,' the romantic Mrs Miller told her daughter one night while brushing her dark, curly hair.

Unfamiliar with this particular expression, the seventeen-year-old became paranoid that her skin was the victim of a host of unsightly blemishes—something that Pádraig had no business in seeing—and so, she didn't leave her bedroom for two whole days. When the teenager and her impeccable skin finally emerged, a letter was waiting for her. As she quickly scanned it, her heart racing, she saw that Pádraig was inviting her to the annual Bealtaine dance in a week. She also noticed that his spelling was abysmal, but her excitement about his delightful request superseded any interest in being pernickety.

'I will bee passen your house at to o'clok this aftarnune when you can give me your anser.'

At two on the dot, Pádraig arrived, visibly nervous. 'Hi,' he said, his voice quivering, his lips trembling.

'Hello, Pádraig,' she replied with absolute confidence; inwardly, her pounding heart was fit to burst from her chest.

Before their exchange could move beyond mere pleasantries, a roar on a par with a cow giving birth was heard from the top of the lane.

'Pádraig! I want you home this minute!'

Butsy's admirer froze to the spot, a look of abject terror hijacking his angelic face.

'Coming, Mother!' he replied, and without even so much as a by-your-leave, Pádraig disappeared, leaving young Miss Miller extremely disappointed but still very much bewitched.

That evening, as Butsy cleared away the dinner plates, Mr Miller noticed that his daughter seemed distracted; even though he had spotted Pádraig fleeing the farm earlier that day, he was yet to make the connection. When Mrs Miller explained the situation to him that night while cutting his toenails, the penny finally dropped for him. He admired his wife's penchant for romance but thought it dangerous to encourage the courtship. The whole county of Meath knew that Mrs Ita Keogh was a harridan, guaranteed to put the kibosh on any dalliance between her only son and an impoverished farmer's daughter. (Ironically, Mrs Keogh had a battalion of spinster daughters who were often confused with their farm animals; as such, the matriarch was finding it impossible to relieve herself of her seven burdens.)

'What do you want me to say to her: "You're not good enough, Butsy"?' Mrs Miller demanded to know, waving the scissors a little too close to the poor man's face.

'That's not what I'm saying, and you know it's not. You always twist my words!'

'Listen to you!' Mrs Miller continued. 'Listen to how ruffled you are. Is it because your "girlfriend" has gone to Navan for the week?'

'Mrs Keane is not my girlfriend—for the hundredth time, I wasn't giving her the wrong impression by throwing a few extra eggs into her order!'

In the end, the pair agreed that it was important for their only child to learn the world's ways on her own. They also decided that there would be no extra eggs thrown into anyone's basket in the future.

* * *

After returning to the convent, Sister Agatha crept up to her cell, where she sat alone for about an hour, stupefied by the day's tragic turn of events. She caught her reflection in the mirror that hung on the wall, and while her face boasted more lines than a rock star's bedside locker, she felt far from being in extremis. She replayed Doctor McManus' words repeatedly, each time hoping that she might have been mistaken somehow. But there seemed to be only one way that 'Ye could give her a week, but I think it's best to put her out of her misery straight away' could be interpreted. Yes, there was no doubt about it: after one hundred and eighteen years, Sister Agatha was finally being asked to leave the dance floor.

15

In the convent, she was affectionately known as the Dustbin—such was her willingness to polish off the leftovers that loitered about the other sisters' plates. ('Where does she put it?' her counterparts continuously questioned.) Having missed lunch, a concerned Sister Josephine popped into the cell to ensure everything was well.

'But it was your favourite—tomato, orange and lentil soup!' the culinary virtuoso argued, unable to accept that the Dustbin had suddenly lost her appetite.

Sister Agatha admitted that the menu would typically leave her taste buds doing a *céile* dance, but today, she just didn't have the stomach for it.

'I'm a little tired after my visit to Doctor McManus, Sister,' she explained. 'Besides, summer is fast approaching, and I want to look as presentable as possible when walking the length and breadth of Bettystown beach in my new swimwear!'

'Is that a fact?' Sister Josephine replied, and even though she wasn't convinced by what she was hearing, the TV addict was desperate to continue watching last night's episode of *Ros na Rún* on the TG4 Player, so she bade farewell and fled to the recreational room.

This brief exchange reminded Sister Agatha of the importance of keeping up her energy—at least until she found a remedy to the problem at hand. Seeing as tomatoes and oranges were ripe with Vitamin C—the perfect thing to invigorate her tired and frail body—she promised to grab herself a bowl later. Her gaze wandered around the compact space. Sister Agatha noted, and not for the first time, how amusing it was that she slept in a cell just like a common criminal. Although, over the years, there were moments where it had felt as if she were carrying out a life-long sentence. Being a messenger of God was not for the fainthearted, that was for sure. But it seemed that a faint heart was exactly what she now possessed.

As of today, Sister Agatha enjoyed the status of being the fifth-oldest person in the world. She had been the recipient of much praise over the past number of years on account of her extraordinary longevity, but the nun had no interest in kind words unless they were said while she was standing on top of that figurative podium clutching onto gold. For many, becoming the world's oldest person might seem like a ridiculous vow, but Sister Agatha was hell-bent on realising it—and not wanting to offend her maker, she couldn't help but get frustrated. It now appeared that she would stumble at the final hurdle. No epitaph ever read: Here lie the remains of the world's fifth-oldest person. No, the history books only mentioned your name if you were the best—not fifth best!

Sister Agatha reached over to the wooden locker, one of the cell's few pieces of furniture, and opened the top drawer before removing a collection of newspaper cut-outs. She laid them out on top of her lumpy bed with delicate precision. They originated from Tunisia, America, Poland and Italy and spotlighted the only four people in the world older than Sister Agatha. Since she had made her improbable vow, the nun kept track of her rivals—the town's library, with its computer and printer, had become a home away from home for her. (*Isn't this WWW lark an absolute marvel?* she had repeatedly mused.)

In recent months, Sister Agatha had become obsessed with this final quartet: where they were from and what their long lives were like. Most importantly, she continuously wondered who was most likely to shed their mortal coils first. By the look of their jolly photographs, it was clear that none had just been told by their equivalent of Doctor McManus that their health was going the way of the Roman Empire. No, she conceded, they weren't leaving anytime soon—at least, not in the next week.

Her chaotic mind then raced ahead to her impending passing, and she started conjuring up vivid pictures of her funeral and burial. Irish wakes were known for their hijinks, where drinks ran free and tongues even more so. Except that wouldn't be the case in approximately one week—or one hour should that wretched Doctor McManus have his way. The final goodbyes for sisters of the Order of Saint Aloysius were private and unfussy affairs—a few prayers, a few hymns and a few sods of earth on the coffin lid, then back to business. Unable to rein in her morbid pessimism, Sister Agatha even doubted that *The Meath Chronicle* or *LMFM* radio station would recognise her extraordinary lifespan.

Sure, why would they? she lamented. *Olympians don't dedicate their lives to push-ups and pull-ups so that they can come fifth.*

No, everybody wanted to be top of the pops, and none more so than Sister Agatha. As she returned her gaze to the clippings, a mischievous idea suddenly manifested in her mind, but she immediately dismissed it: it was too sensational, ridiculous, and impossible.

Or was it?

* * *

Every year, on the first day of May, the festival of Bealtaine took place to mark the beginning of summer, when the cattle were driven out to stretch their legs and have a spot of fun in the pastures. To protect the livestock and crops and ensure that everything grew as it should, many outlandish rituals were carried out across the country, such as lighting bonfires or placing yellow flowers on these cows. Not only did the community of Kilberry perform all of these age-old traditions with enthusiasm, but they also went one better and organised an annual fair—complete with singing, dancing and plenty of night-time tomfoolery.

Festivities were due to kick off in the specially erected marquee at eight, so at seven, Butsy got dressed to the nines. Since Pádraig had been abruptly summoned away from her house the week previously, he had proven himself to be remarkably adept at keeping details of their blossoming relationship from his mother. Over the following days, Liam, the local creamery owner, delivered Pádraig's romantic—if, at times, incomprehensible—love letters when visiting the Millers' farm to collect empty milk bottles. Pádraig had assured Butsy that Mrs Keogh wouldn't be anywhere near the dance because she had an important engagement in Dublin that night. (The dutiful mother was expected to meet the elderly Lord and Lady Dunsany to convince their son to take one of her seven daughters as his bride. That this bachelor was forty years older than her youngest was inconsequential, she had previously assured the Dunsanys.)

Pádraig's final correspondence to Butsy stated that they would meet under the large sycamore tree in the field behind the church before walking into the marquee 'to getter'. With the help of the bright red bow that her parents had gifted her for a recent birthday, Butsy succeeded in bringing order to her wild curls. She had also borrowed a pretty lilac dress from the mother of her friend, Sissy Stapleton, and attached a bunch of pretty bluebells to the lapel. Mr Miller thought that she was the most delightful creature he had seen since Mrs Miller had walked up the aisle all those years ago; Butsy herself thought she looked presentable— nothing more, nothing less.

As she raced towards the sycamore tree, deftly sidestepping the mounds of manure that littered the fields, she could not prevent herself from imagining all the different outcomes of the night. In her favourite role-play, they both stood in front of the refreshment bar. As soon as they finished some drink or other, he would take the empty glass from her hand before swooping in for a passionate kiss! Oh, if only a wind would introduce itself and help her get to the sycamore tree a little bit quicker! (Actually, maybe just a light breeze; anything stronger would wreak havoc with her hair, she suddenly realised.)

When she neared the meeting point and saw him, kitted out in a ridiculous, ill-fitting suit, Butsy knew she would never love another man as much as she loved Pádraig Keogh. She stopped in front of him, and this time it was her turn to be stumped. Being a gentleman, he saved her from her blushes and simply held his hand aloft and asked, 'May I dance with the most beautiful girl in all of Kilberry?'

Even though there were only about twenty girls in the entire village, seven of whom were his unsightly sisters, she thought it best to take the compliment rather than question it.

'Yes, you may.'

As expected, the marquee was black with people—some were behaving like the beacons of society; some were not. But, as soon as the young lovebirds took to the floor, the large crowd did like Moses and the Red Sea and parted to the sides to have a good gawk at love's young dream. (Creamery Liam had not been as discreet as Pádraig had hoped and told the whole village about the blossoming romance.) But, at that moment, the two darlings could have been all alone, such was the enchantment between them, and they danced as if they were beating from the same heart.

The heart belonging to Pádraig's mother, who had just arrived at the marquee unannounced, did not beat. Instead, it was like a gigantic iceberg similar to the one that bothered the *Titanic* three years earlier. And just like the ship on that fateful night, Mrs Keogh was there to ensure that any designs the peasant girl had on her darling son sank without a trace. (Yes, it became apparent that Liam owned not only the parish's biggest creamery but also its biggest mouth.)

'Get your greedy hands off him!' Mrs Keogh yelled at Butsy. When the teenager refused to comply—out of shock rather than insolence—the furious woman bolted across the wooden floor. 'Are you deaf as well as dirty? Get off him, I said!'

Pádraig's attempts to diffuse the situation were in vain; as most people knew, once Irish mammies had gotten something into her head, there was no talking to them, so their children would be best served saving their breath to cool their potatoes.

'Don't you dare question me, ye pup! Just wait until I get you home!' She dragged him from the hall, ending the best bit of drama to grace the village since it emerged that Mrs Maguire's baby bore a striking resemblance to the local bachelor schoolteacher.

When Butsy returned home, she slumped onto her bed and curled up into a ball. Just as she was about to scold herself for being so naïve and silly, a series of pebbles crashed against her window. She jumped up and pulled the curtains, unsure if she had imagined things. But there in front of her stood the last person she expected to see: Pádraig, sweat dripping from his brow. He struggled to catch his breath, having run from his house several miles away, he soon explained.

'You shouldn't be here, Pád—'

'Shhh, listen,' he ordered. 'If you took every star from that sky tonight and multiplied them by every blade of grass in this field, that figure would only be a fraction of how much I love you, Butsy Miller.'

He placed both of his clammy hands against the windowpane. 'Pack a bag and meet me under the sycamore tree at six o'clock in the morning. Liam will drive us to Dublin, where we will marry in the afternoon. Afterwards, we'll be able to dance together forever. Well, until we tire of it, I suppose.'

He moved closer, and even though his heavy breathing now clouded the glass between them, Butsy could see the fierce passion in his eyes. He then removed a ring from his pocket, complete with the largest emerald that she was sure ever existed. Butsy prayed that her racing heart wouldn't burst from within and sully the moment.

'I'm told that this jewel was Cleopatra's favourite and is known as the stone of successful love,' he revealed. 'I've also heard mention that emerald is a symbol of growth and the future.'

And with that, Pádraig got down on one knee. 'Butsy Miller, will you grow with me every single day into the future?'

The idealistic farmer's daughter had entertained a profusion of fantasies about how the night would play out, but a marriage proposal was a little ambitious, even by her romantic standards.

'Well?' he asked, seeing as Butsy hadn't said a word for almost a minute.

'Yes, yes, yes!' she finally replied, hopping out of the window. There followed an intense embrace; no interfering mother interrupted them this time.

'See you at six,' Pádraig called out as he disappeared across the field.

'See you at six.'

* * *

It hadn't taken Sister Agatha long to gather her belongings, seeing as the Order's vow of poverty ensured fashion was always unfashionable amongst the nuns. Bag packed, she scanned her cell for what would probably be the very last time. She didn't feel any sadness or finality—she was far too preoccupied with the mission at hand.

While her age had often been described as monumental, the one-hundred-and-eighteen-year-old's experience as a traveller left a lot to be desired—despite showing interest in far-flung places as a curious schoolgirl. As it happened, she had only ventured out of the Royal County of Meath on a handful of occasions: the Eucharistic Congress of 1932 and 2012; Pope John Paul's visit in 1979; and that time when Sister Assumpta's life-long battle with alcoholism had gotten the better of her, and she ended up on a stag-do in Valentia Island off the coast of Kerry. (Sister Agatha, along with some tight-lipped nuns, had to travel to the Kingdom to retrieve her. Luckily, the tattoo that Sister Assumpta had been unwittingly gifted went unnoticed by everyone—except her gynaecologist.) Other than that, Sister Agatha's motherland was alien to her, and as for the rest of the world—well, England may have been a different planet.

It wasn't that the church frowned on its members taking an excursion here or there; it was just that being single-minded by nature, Sister Agatha had always felt duty-bound to remain in situ. Her direction in life had changed since her early, wanderlust years and had naturally evolved into one that didn't involve bouts of jet lag or the crossing of choppy waters. Instead, she saw the world and its glory in the parishioners she met daily—even the long-winded ones—and that suited her. Until now.

Luckily, every nun at the Order of Saint Aloysius was equipped with a passport on the off-chance, they joked, that they received an invitation to the Vatican. (The ladies in Saint Bartholomew's in County Tipperary had received precisely that in the mid-50s in recognition of their philanthropic duties in the community—an honour that proved to be a contentious issue amongst the other convents. 'Anyone could plant a few flowers and clean a bit of graffiti off some back-alley walls.')

Sister Agatha dusted off her unused passport and, armed with good old-fashioned determination, crept out of the convent while the other nuns slept soundly. (Sister Imelda's snoring usually kept the others wide awake—sinus problems were the curse of the devil; it had been repeatedly noted. But her widowed cousin was in the throes of depression owing to a botched haircut, so Sister Imelda was comforting her—much to the delight of the sleep-deprived nuns.)

Just as the sun made its first appearance of the day, Sister Agatha walked through the immaculately maintained gardens towards the front gate but suddenly stopped. The large, wooden cross looming above the entrance reminded her of the morally dubious nature of her plan. Even though Saint Peter would surely have stern words with her in a week, she knew this was her last opportunity to fulfil her vow.

Yes, there is no other option.

After waving to her sleeping companions, she headed for the bus stop. There, she would start a journey that would see her carrying out a deed that was illegal in every single country in the world.

* * *

When Butsy had raced across the same fields the evening before, she was convinced that her two feet would never experience such speed again. That was merely a trot compared to the pace with which she sprinted to the sycamore tree on the morning of her wedding – despite being weighed down by a large valise and an even larger engagement ring. Her parents had given their blessing to the hastily concocted plan on the promise that the young couple immediately return to Kilberry after saying 'I do'. There wasn't much Mrs Keogh could do then, they concluded. Mrs Miller had even helped her daughter pack, giving her the simple wedding dress she had worn all those decades ago when marrying Butsy's father.

Ever thrifty, Mrs Miller had been delighted to realise that the dress covered both the 'something old' and 'something borrowed' parts of a recent, popular custom. Better again, thanks to the hem's colourful pattern, the 'something blue' had also been ticked off the list. The 'something new' had taken the form of a beautiful garland that Mrs Miller put together from a collection of recently sprung flowers.

As Butsy approached the meeting point, she was surprised

to see so many people there (blabbermouth Liam, up to his old tricks again). But the one person who was missing was Pádraig, although she was prevented from dwelling on this worriment, too busy fielding kind words from her neighbours.

'There won't be another bride to match your beauty!'

'You'll have ten children, I'll bet!'

'It will be the happiest of homes, that's for sure!'

The well-wishers were so excited about the forthcoming nuptials that nobody noticed that it was well after six and Pádraig had yet to arrive. Butsy did not give up hope.

He will be here; I know he will, she thought, confident that there was no way her fiancé would abandon her in front of the entire community for a second time.

Mr Carmody, the local undertaker, suddenly hushed the crowd. In the distance, he spotted a figure walking in their direction. 'It's him; I'm sure it is!'

Everyone turned and held their breath. While the person approaching was not dissimilar to Pádraig, Butsy immediately knew that it wasn't the love of her life—this person's frame was too slender, his walk too heavy. Soon, everyone realised that it was the Keogh's stable boy, Fiach.

'I've a message for Butsy,' the fourteen-year-old announced as he reached the gathering, his voice yet to break.

'He's not coming, is he?' she stuttered, desperately trying—and failing—to keep her emotions in check.

When Fiach shook his head, everyone let out a long, disappointed cry.

'The fecker!'

'The bastard!'

'I'll ring his ears!'

Butsy said nothing. Instead, as the others cursed the no-show, the grief-stricken teenager discreetly broke away from the crowd and hurried home with a mangled heart and her mother's unworn wedding dress. This time, she didn't pay a blind bit of notice to the endless cowpats she had been so keen to avoid the night before.

* * *

Before Saint Agatha of Sicily had become Saint Agatha of Sicily, she was a simple fifteen-year-old girl from a wealthy and noble family. Being a devout Christian, the teenager dedicated her virginity to God. When Quintianus, a low-born Roman prefect, tried to have his wicked way with her, Agatha immediately rejected his unwanted advances. Furious and bruised, the arrogant louse then persecuted the youngster for her impenetrable faith and sent her to a brothel to teach her a lesson.

Despite this challenging environment, Agatha proved to be intractable. So, ever the gentleman, Quintianus went one step further and imprisoned her—a decision that didn't faze her in the slightest. Galled by her resilience, Quintianus then subjected the renegade to an endless onslaught of torture, culminating in Agatha's breasts being violently cut off with pincers. But she remained steadfast and refused to recant. As such, the girl was sentenced to be burned at the stake.

Thanks to an earthquake, Agatha was spared and sent back to prison. There, it was thought that Saint Peter the Apostle appeared and healed her wounds. Depending on who was telling the story, Agatha died in prison sometime around her twentieth birthday, a virgin martyr.

Butsy Miller had always been aware of Saint Agatha's story as her birthday had fallen on the Sicilian's Memorial Day, but it was only after the unfortunate incident under the sycamore tree that Butsy, looking for inspiration anywhere she could find it, properly read up on the saint's fate and immediately empathised with her. Here was another female whose life had also been destroyed at the hands of a brute of a man. Of course, on paper, Pádraig couldn't hold a candle to Quintianus, but in the immediate aftermath of his betrayal, broken-hearted and embarrassed, Butsy had been convinced that he was worse—far worse. After several weeks, when there was still no sign of Pádraig, she had found great solace and fortitude in Saint Agatha's story and would spend hours talking to the late rabble-rouser, positive that they were kindred spirits.

Suspicious that their only child was no longer of sound mind

('Seán, she's talking to the wall again'), her parents were on the verge of sending for the local doctor.

'I'm fine,' Butsy reassured them. 'I'm more than fine - I'm going to become a nun and take the name of my heroine and dear friend, Saint Agatha.'

While it was common for young men and women to follow a life of prayer at that time, initially, Butsy's parents had been doubtful that their once-spirited daughter would be able to meet a convent's strict demands. Secretly, Mr and Mrs Miller had hoped that after time had passed and wounds had healed, Butsy would return to her buoyant self (and give those poor walls a little peace!). Oh, how they underestimated the doggedness of their only child, who stuck to a decision once she made it.

The Millers' fears for Butsy's impetuous decision proved unfounded: the moment she entered the Order of Saint Aloysius, the young novice thrived. Perhaps on account of never having any siblings, she relished the idea of being surrounded by so many sisters while also fully embracing the solidarity that went hand-in-hand with convent life.

Admittedly, over the first few months, she had often thought of Pádraig. One night, and not for the first time in her life, she was awoken by the sound of pebbles being thrown at her window. For a split second, she had hoped that it was her old flame. It turned out to be Sister Angelica, who had locked herself out after disobeying the convent's rules not to feed the stray cats.

Sister Agatha wondered what she would have said or done if it had been Pádraig outside her cell as she returned to sleep. Butsy Miller's life had taken a new direction since they had been sweethearts, and things had worked out for the best. Yes, she was sure of it. But why was she disappointed when it was Sister Angelica, covered from head to toe in manky cat hair, who stood outside instead?

She placed her hand underneath her pillow and allowed her hand to rest on the one thing that both she and Cleopatra loved more than anything else in the world. The emerald ring.

* * *

Sister Agatha waited at the bus stop, alone. It gave her time to ensure she was making the right decision. Her mind was akin to a game of tennis, thoughts going back and forth at a speedy pace, but she always returned to the same conclusion: *This is the only way left to fulfil my vow.*

In the distance, she spotted a taxi approaching; her heart stopped. The Meath flag waving on the bonnet meant that her faithful driver, Paul, had started his morning shift. She ducked behind the bin and prayed that he wouldn't notice her.

'Is that you, Sister Agatha?' he shouted, pulling over.

'Oh, is that you, Paul?' she replied, hiding her frustrations that he had just blown her cover.

'What are you doing out at this hour? You'll catch your death!'

Why is everyone obsessed with my demise? she wondered, emerging from her inadequate hiding place.

'Well? What are you doing?'

Unsure of what to say or do, Sister Agatha rifled through the bin.

'Eh, I accidentally threw something away the other day, and I was hoping that I would be able to retrieve it,' she bluffed—the best excuse she could invent under the circumstances.

'Let me help you then,' he suggested, turning the engine off.

'No need! I found it!' She pulled out the first thing she could get her hands on—a rotten banana peel, complete with a dirty cigarette stub and a mound of masticated chewing gum.

'Is that a... banana peel?'

'Yes. Yes, it is.'

Paul looked at her suspiciously.

'Eh, I foolishly threw it away yesterday when, of course, I should have added it to the compost heap in the convent,' Sister Agatha continued. 'The Order of Saint Aloysius is very green, you see.'

'Right,' he replied, accepting for the first time that his friend's health was now in decline.

'Let me drop you home, Sister, seeing as you've found what you're looking for.'

'Don't be daft, Paul; you go off and make some money. I want something extra special for Christmas, so you're going to have to start saving now!'

But Paul wasn't going anywhere other than the hospital, where he would ask the doctors to give his one-hundred-and-eighteen-year-old friend a complete check-up.

'Why don't you get into the car, Sister? It will only take me a minute.'

Based on the condescending tone he was now adopting, Sister Agatha knew that Paul thought she was fit for the sanatorium and needed to act quickly and efficiently for her master plan to prosper.

'Paul,' she said, taking his hand, 'the truth is, at my age, you don't know how many sunrises you have left. And even though the Mother Superior would be furious if she discovered that I was out and about at this hour, I just couldn't resist.'

She pointed towards a dazzling sunrise peeping out above a grove of oak trees to support her claims.

'Isn't it only magnificent?' she said—something that was, most definitely, not a lie.

Paul nodded.

'You won't give the game away, will you?'

Paul released a sigh of relief, smiled, and returned to the car. 'My lips are zipped, Sister. Be sure not to catch a chill, though—it's still only March!'

While Sister Agatha took no pride in telling an untruth, particularly to loyal friends, there was little else she could have done under the circumstances. Thankfully, the bus arrived before anybody else could stumble across her. Anxious to keep to the timetable, the driver decided to overlook any pleasantries and, without so much as a 'good morning', took Sister Agatha's bag and assisted her onboard. This blunt approach suited the bus' lone passenger; it was time to focus the mind, and idle chatter with strangers would only distract her. After taking her seat, Sister Agatha looked out at Navan and surveyed the empty roads and sleeping houses. Soon, the town would be alive with activity; for now, it seemed as if it were conspiring on her behalf, allowing its most adored resident to slip away unnoticed.

From under her habit, she fished out the rosary beads that hung around her neck. Swinging from the bottom was not a cross, as would be standard practice, but instead, a sparkling emerald ring. She clutched onto it tightly and closed her eyes.

'I'm doing this for you, dear heart,' she whispered. 'It's the only way.'

With that, the bus sped across the lush plains of Meath on its way to Dublin Airport. This journey marked the very start of her Herculean mission to complete the vow she made many decades ago. Over the coming week, Sister Agatha would travel to three continents and visit the only four people who were preventing her from being the oldest person in the world.

And then, one by one, she would kill them.

THREE

THE HEALTH & WEALTH BLOG, SPRING 2016

As all our regular readers know, the Health & Wealth team is currently travelling the length and breadth of North Africa, unearthing unique, natural remedies—from shingles to sunburn to sciatica. It was today, in stunning Tunisia, when we struck gold.

Making our way towards the Sahara Desert, we stumbled across a modern-day Florence Nightingale who delighted in sharing her arsenal of medical secrets with us. As proof of the potions' merits, the healer is currently the continent's oldest person, having racked up an extraordinary one-hundred-and-twenty-years so far. And by the looks of things, Tayri Chakchouk isn't planning on calling it a day anytime soon! Surrounded by close to two hundred relatives, this national treasure has plenty of gasoline left in the engine, folks!

And now, thanks to Tayri's remarkable kindness, you can get insights into how best to make old bones. We'll be uploading her remedies once we get a better Wi-Fi connection.

P.S: Unfortunately, we've yet to find a lasting cure for Bob's smelly armpits!

* * *

Sister Agatha was surprised by how quickly her bus reached Dublin Airport, some fifty-four kilometres away. So brief was the journey that the soon-to-be assassin didn't have ample time to explore the specifics of her challenge. What she did manage to decide was to commence her campaign of carnage in reverse order, starting with Tayri Chakchouk.

According to *Le Temps*, one of Tunisia's national newspapers, Tayri lay claim to eighteen children, forty-nine grandchildren, one-hundred-and-twenty great-grandchildren, and seven great-great-grandchildren. Born and raised outside Kebili, an oasis situated on the edge of the Sahara Desert, her story—like those of Howard Hawks, F. Scott Fitzgerald, and the monarch-wrecking Wallis Simpson—started in 1896. Despite being a one-woman maternity hospital since then, she recently celebrated her hundred-and-twentieth birthday, cementing her position as the fourth-oldest person in the world. When Tayri wasn't taking care of her large family, she pursued her other passion: home remedies.

Well, I have the perfect cure for her reluctance to renounce life! the nun joked, now getting carried away by the task at hand.

She descended the bus, quickly retrieved her baggage, and strutted towards the airport entrance with a fine kick in her step. Even though it was just seven o'clock, the building was alive with activity. Sister Agatha couldn't help but get swept away by the intrepid spirit of those dashing about, suitcases in hand. However, the sight of so many giddy friends and families turned her initial cheeriness into sadness. While she had justified the need to disregard the sacred Fifth Commandment, seeing as it was the only feasible way to fulfil her vow, Sister Agatha now struggled to justify swiping the convent's for-emergencies-only Debit Card to do so.

At present, the Order of Saint Aloysius had robust funds following a successful fundraiser to get Sister Josephine a new kitchen. (The talented cook had been making do with an ancient, barely functioning gas cooker while the fridge door hadn't properly closed since John F. Kennedy was still in office.) And now, Sister Agatha was on the verge of betraying her dear comrades, who were more than just fellow sisters; they were also sisters. But this light-fingered indiscretion was a necessary evil, she now firmly reminded her conscience - after all, the nun wasn't going to travel the world on her good looks alone, was she?

Sister Josephine is that good a chef, she could whip up a feast using the sun as her only heat, she assured herself, her wrist receiving a wallop. She certainly needed to toughen up if her naughty plan was to prosper.

With those pesky, self-righteous inner voices silenced—for the time being at least—there was nothing left for Sister Agatha to do but take a flight to Tunisia and eliminate an over-zealous child-bearer named Tayri Chakchouk.

Do I pay the pilot as I board the plane, or is there a ticket-seller I should consult first?

* * *

Growing up, Wayne Farrell's older brother was an out-and-out scoundrel. To ridicule the acne that massacred the impressionable teenager's face, his sibling had christened him Pepperoni Pizza. Years later, Wayne's acne had, mercifully, disappeared, but the memory of that traumatic time lingered; the twenty-four-year-old battled with self-esteem, especially when it came to members of the fairer sex.

Even though women constantly surrounded him thanks to his job as an information provider at Dublin Airport, Wayne invariably went bright red or perspired when in their company. He assured himself that things would improve with time, but if the number of deodorant cans he put away was anything to go by, that optimistic prognosis remained out of reach. His only comfort was that he didn't work in a factory plucking chickens like his hateful older brother.

Wayne's position at the airport was one he had held for over two years, but it wasn't those intimidating, sweat-inducing ladies alone who required his services. He was often approached by many larger-than-life characters who would probably feel more at home in an asylum than at an airport. Although, this morning was the first time a disorientated nun, who might have been alive before aviation was even invented, came looking for assistance.

'I want to go to Kebili,' she informed him while shovelling their complimentary hardboiled sweets into her mouth.

Wayne didn't know how to deal with the situation. Had this elderly nun wandered out of a nursing home and was now unable to find her way back to her lodgings? Rather than a flight to Kebili, was she looking for a taxi to Cabra, perhaps? Should he alert security or his manager at the very least? But these musings were interrupted by Ravishing Rita, his beautiful colleague who stole both his lunch and heart on a daily basis. She had just arrived to work thirty minutes late—something else she regularly did.

'Tryin' to get to Kebili, are ye, love?' she asked. 'A spontaneous holiday, is it? Good for you.'

Luckily Ravishing Rita wasn't afflicted with the same ageist outlook as her once-spotty co-worker and immediately set to work assisting this adorable old dame who was happily stuffing her face—and pockets—with confectionery. Blessed with beauty, Rita hadn't been gifted with brains and didn't have a bog's notion where this Kebili place was located. Luckily for Sister Agatha, she excelled in computer searches, and as soon as she sent Wayne to fetch her a coffee and breakfast bap, Rita discovered that this sweet-toothed nun was en route to Tunisia.

'There's no direct flights, hun, so your best bet is to first hop on a plane to Paris and change there for Tunis. It'll be a long auld trek, but I'm sure it'll be worth it. You'll come back with a gorgeous colour, I bet.'

Seeing as Rita had something of an eye for Jean-Pierre at Air France, she insisted on taking her new friend over to him to arrange the flights—an act that proved highly lucrative for all involved. Sister Agatha was upgraded to first-class ('*Alors*, a friend of Ravishing Rita, is a friend of mine!') while Rita bagged herself a date for Saturday night.

Yes, the brief exchange was profitable for all—except for poor Wayne, who was left holding a breakfast bap and mug of coffee that were, just like his love life, getting colder by the minute.

* * *

Airport security officer Yvonne Goodchild always argued that it was easier for a single father to secure love than a single mother— where a man's stock soared, a woman's plummeted. The thirty-five-year-old redhead had been on every dating website imaginable in her quest to find someone to share her life with—one that consisted of four children, all under the age of ten. On dates, Yvonne would openly admit that life was tough, and the bills were relentless—information that had, unsurprisingly, proven quite unattractive for potential wooers so far.

Recently, it looked as if her ship had finally come in when, after many frogs, Yvonne met her prince. Or so she thought. Derek was attractive, wealthy, an excellent listener, and smelled like a summer's meadow. But when she arrived home one night after a long day at the airport, she discovered him sitting at her kitchen table, filling out forms for the boarding school where he intended on sending her four small children.

'It doesn't matter if Jeff is only ten months old—they accept all ages!' he had argued.

Yvonne knew there and then that her relationship with this prince wouldn't have a happy ending. After Derek had packed his bags, Yvonne decided that the only solution to her financial difficulties was to work as hard as she could, get a promotion, and pay her own wretched bills.

This morning, when she spotted a shifty, bespectacled nun in line for the security check, Yvonne felt positive that she was on the verge of capturing a shyster, thereby inching her way up the career ladder. Drug smugglers dressed as nuns or priests were an old joke amongst employees at security checks the world over; after Yvonne noticed this person, kitted out in the full regalia, looking uncomfortable and unsure, the mother-of-four went in for the kill. When the suspect passed through the metal detectors, Yvonne wasn't surprised that the alarms didn't sound—after all, criminals were masterful at overcoming almost all obstacles the civilised world put in their way. But most criminals had not come across the razor-sharp Yvonne Goodchild.

'I'm going to have to do a body search, I'm afraid,' she informed the woman, taking her to one side.

Yvonne's initial investigations got off to a crummy start when she realised that her handheld metal detector was being temperamental once again.

How is someone supposed to shine when they are allocated such inadequate equipment? she frequently asked herself.

The career-hungry officer had to excuse herself and search for a functioning detector. When she returned, Yvonne simply expected her catch-of-the-day to have her arms and legs outstretched.

However, the woman was busy disrobing, inspired by the other passengers removing their shoes and belts. But she didn't just take off her black loafers. Moments later, she proudly stood in front of everyone, almost as naked as the day she was born—which clearly wasn't yesterday or the day before. With no attempts to preserve her modesty, the woman placed her hands on her hips, stuck out her tongue, and proceeded to reel off a series of 'Aaahs' as if she were undergoing a doctor's examination!

The peculiar scene emboldened all the other travellers, and a cacophony of whoops and hollers followed. Even Yvonne's po-faced colleagues were getting in on the act, unable to resist a good giggle to break the monotony of the day. Having realised the error of her way ('She is a bloody nun!'), Yvonne quickly handed the elderly woman her habit and veil, along with all the other items of clothing scattered across the ground. At the same time, she insisted that a voyeuristic teenager delete the footage he had taken of the incident from his mobile phone. Uncertain of how to best remedy the situation, Yvonne led the naked sister into a nearby room to give her privacy and a refreshing cup of tea.

'Please accept my deepest apologies, Sister,' Yvonne pleaded, hoping such contrite words and a couple of Hob Nobs would quench any desire for this poor passenger to lodge a formal complaint.

But the security officer's attempts at atonement appeared to have been unnecessary because as the nun dressed ('You couldn't help me with my zip, dear?'), she talked a blue streak about how much she was looking forward to an adventure of a lifetime.

'If I have time, I'll send you a postcard somewhere along the way,' she added, popping the entire packet of biscuits into her bag.

The magnanimous lady tottered off into the terminal, drawing a line under the whole embarrassing affair. Suppose Yvonne's detector had been working in the first place, all of this could have been avoided, she thought, giving credence to that old proverb that a workwoman always blames her tools.

* * *

Sister Agatha had never been airborne before, but she was, of course, familiar with the concept of flying. While she hadn't been around when Leonardo Da Vinci made sketches of parachutes and helicopters in the sixteenth century, she vividly remembered all the hoo-ha about the Wright Brothers and their aviation accomplishments when she was just a child.

('It will never take off,' her father said of the whole enterprise at the time, with the young girl unsure whether he was being cynical or making a joke; he loved his puns.)

However familiar she was with the workings of a plane, nothing could have prepared Sister Agatha for the electrifying feeling of flying, looking out the window and seeing Dublin's beautiful coastline grow smaller and smaller before vanishing under the clouds altogether. For the first ten minutes after leaving the runway, this fledgeling's mouth remained so firmly open, a swarm of bees could have easily taken up residency within. (Luckily, Air France had an exemplary hygiene policy.)

What most surprised Sister Agatha was that she appeared to be the only person on board who was awestruck by the process; the other passengers around her were either flicking through magazines or had fallen into a deep slumber. Yes, she had less than a week left to live, but the nun was emphatic that she would never tire of this magical experience if her life continued for another ten centuries.

Thanks to Jean-Pierre, Wayne's rival for Ravishing Rita's affections, this first-time flyer enjoyed her maiden voyage in the best possible light. There was plenty of room to stretch her legs, a blanket should she get cold, and a pillow if she cared to drift off during the short flight (she didn't).

'Would you like a glass of champagne, Sister?' a soft-spoken air hostess inquired—an offer that allowed this passenger to tick off another box that morning: getting drunk.

Having barely eaten a morsel since Doctor McManus had dropped the bombshell the morning before, Sister Agatha had a stomach that needed filling, and the best remedy she could come up with was to throw the contents of the flute into her quick smart. And when that had vanished, a second, then third, helping was requested.

'Another drop?' she innocently asked.

Being the fifth-oldest person in the world, hungry and unaccustomed to the ritual of drinking, one didn't need to be a detective to deduce that Sister Agatha would soon find herself three sheets to the wind.

And the flight hadn't yet cleared the Irish Sea.

* * *

Fergal Kenny had always been an impossible person. In his early years, he had repeatedly broken his mother's heart as she tried to convince—or bribe—him to eat his greens or go to bed on time. His harried teachers had counted down the days until the summer holidays so that they could be free of the insolent brat who never did a lick of work in his entire school life. The few girlfriends he indulged for short bursts had been left with an embarrassment of insecurities and bad memories, and no amount of therapy could erase the damage.

Such a disagreeable disposition stood him in good stead in the subsequent years as he ruthlessly clambered to the top of the corporate ladder, making light work of anyone who had the misfortune of getting in his way. If it hadn't been for the recession of 2008, which saw his company's shares plummet, Fergal would undoubtedly have become the natural heir to the thrones of Franco or Mussolini. As it was, he remained insufferable; he just no longer had the funds to pull it off as successfully as those halcyon days.

For Fergal, one of the most distressing aspects of being bankrupt was how he was forced to travel. Having spent years being fawned over by beautiful air hostesses in First Class, he had now been relegated to Economy—and today was proving itself to be one of his worst experiences yet. The woman next to him had whipped out her right breast, from which her three-month-old baby was happily feeding.

What is the world coming to? he questioned despairingly.

He pulled an air steward's shirt and let his thoughts on such immodesty be known.

'You can go sing if you think I'm sitting beside this shite!' Fergal roared, ensuring that everyone on board became embroiled in the dispute.

Ignoring protests from the cabin crew, Fergal rose to his feet and stormed up the aisle into the sanctuary of First Class. Here, he discovered that the only seat available was beside a nun but concluded that anything was better than the lewdness in Economy.

Peace at last.

Or so he thought. Having imbibed a few sploshes of champagne, the nun, who had just overheard his offensive comments, decided that someone needed to be taken down a peg or two.

'Maybe you'll be so kind as to enlighten me,' the sister probed, trying valiantly not to slur her words. 'How can someone—as bald as an eggshell with a belly the size of the Sugar Loaf Mountain—have such a high opinion of himself?'

(As he tried to ignore her, Fergal decided there and then that despite being in the red, he was booking himself in for a hair restoration treatment when he returned from Paris.)

'You are clearly unaware of the birds and the bees and that a mother nursing her child is the most natural experience on earth. A woman's breasts aren't just there for your enjoyment; they're there to nurture and feed.'

Fergal closed his eyes and tried to imagine that he was in his happy place—or indeed any place other than where he was: sitting beside a drunken, geriatric nun who was shouting about the machinations of a pair of tits! To add insult to injury, she seemed in no hurry to end her ravings and proceeded to give him the A-to-Z on how people should treat others, notably new mothers ('respect and kindness,' blah, blah, blah).

Fergal received additional advice from the crowd that had now formed around him – including how not to be a 'prick' (the woman who hurled that particular insult looked vaguely familiar to him; was she a scorned former lover, perhaps?). Just as it looked as if the dispute would never find a resolution, the nun's face suddenly blanched whiter than the clouds outside. Before anyone could even inquire about her health, she vomited all over Fergal's cream chinos before crashing out on his shoulders. Suddenly, Economy didn't seem as unpleasant to Fergal as he had initially thought.

38

* * *

When Sister Agatha awoke sometime later, a staff member from Air France held her aloft on the back of a buggy, which happily zipped through Charles de Gaulle Airport. As her connecting flight to Tunisia was due to board just moments after she had landed in the French capital, the ever-accommodating Jean-Pierre had made prior arrangements for his VIP passenger to get transported from one terminal to the other.

The nun thought her head seemed a little troubled; in fact, it pounded. She didn't want to imagine what it would have felt like without the assistance of her tinted glasses. Her last memory was quaffing some champagne while chatting to the brute sitting next to her. After that, nothing—a complete blank. It wasn't just upstairs that was running amok; her stomach had experienced better days, too.

'How are you feeling, *Soeur*?' the staff member probed, a glint in his eye. '*Mon Dieu*, I believe you put on quite a show on the flight!'

Sister Agatha didn't know how to reply. Should there be an admission that she was entirely in the dark about what 'show" she had performed while airborne? Or should she pretend that she was in control of her actions and everything said and done had been fully intended? In the end, there wasn't any time to reply as they had reached their destination.

'*Au revoir*,' the jolly, if somewhat pass-remarkable, employee yelled after assisting his passenger onto one of the seats outside her gate.

Boarding was only minutes away, but Sister Agatha wished it were longer. In front of a nearby gate, a troupe of fabulous can-can dancers entertained fellow passengers as they waited for their flight to Warsaw, a city where, all going well, Sister Agatha would be visiting in only a matter of days. Possibly still inebriated, she became swept away by the enchanting charms of the three voluptuous ladies and couldn't resist tapping her feet and shuffling in her seat. As the music began to build, Sister Agatha now felt a sudden urge to get up and join in the merriment. Even though

Doctor McManus had offered a pessimistic outlook on her health, hangover aside, the nun felt more vital than ever.

Her flight was now boarding, so if she were going to seize the day, Sister Agatha needed to do it right at that minute.

'Hump it!' she declared before jumping up.

But that was as far as her escapades went; the sudden rush to become vertical did not go down well with her fragile stomach. The delicious Moët that she had inhaled earlier that morning made a second, unexpected re-appearance—although, this time, it took a different and even more unfortunate exit route.

FOUR

On the day of her First Holy Communion, the raven-haired Sister Fidelma was introduced to the joys of gambling. After she and her classmates had allowed the delicious wafer to melt on their tongues, her mother returned home from the church to prepare a special lunch while her father, who owned a travelling confectionery store, whisked the youngster away to Navan Racecourse. Here, he hoped to sell an avalanche of chocolate bars from the back of his van—as luck would have it, a dazzling sun was perched high in the sky on that April afternoon, so punters happily treated themselves to Mr Duggan's wares. (*Thank God*, he thought, *I could almost have bought a second van with the money I spent on that flippin' First Holy Communion dress!*)

On seeing young Sister Fidelma—or Noni Duggan, as she was then known—one of her father's generous customers gave her a shilling in recognition of her momentous day.

'Don't spend it all in one shop,' the kind man joked before heading off to squander what he had just inherited from a late aunt.

Her father was up to high doh selling sweets and chocolate, so Noni decided to have an adventure and disappeared into the crowds. Wandering about, she became transfixed by the striking fashion on show. After endless decades cowering behind layers of fabrics, Irish women finally cast off the excess during the sixties, revealing that these Celtic colleens did have legs—and often quite lovely ones.

One such outfit that caught Noni's attention was a bold red pinafore, perfectly matched with cream tights and funky platform

41

shoes. The trendy young woman who wore the ensemble was too busy puffing a cigarette to notice Noni's admiring gaze. While she claimed just seven short years, Noni was worldly enough to know that the solitary shilling she clutched tightly in her hand would not be sufficient for her to afford a similar outfit. If only she had been as disciplined as her younger brother, who had actually made use of the piggy bank that Santa Claus had given them each at Christmas.

After wracking her mind for a remedy, Noni finally stumbled across the ideal solution to her financial woes. Apart from the latest trends, the seemingly angelic girl also noticed that people were scurrying towards kiosks then receiving large sums of money for their troubles. They looked too old to have just made their First Holy Communion, so why were they being gifted all those notes? Was it as easy as walking up to one and asking those within for money? 'Nothing ventured, nothing gained' was something her grandmother often said, so Noni decided it was best to take heed of such sagacity and cautiously approached one.

A man, whose cheeks were almost as red as his fiery hair, stuck his head out of the little window. He appeared stressed, and Noni doubted that he was someone who would dole out money willy-nilly.

'I would like to buy a dress, but I don't think I have enough money. May I have some?' she asked, without holding out too much hope.

Noni's instinct soon transpired to be spot-on. The bookmaker wasn't in any mood for silly little girls; not only had his wife burnt his breakfast that morning, but he also just lost a small fortune thanks to some gammy-legged horse defeating the odds and emerging triumphant.

'How much do you have?' he barked, one hand outstretched, the other clutching onto a pair of rosary beads, praying that his luck would change.

Noni held the single shilling in front of her. While the bookmaker hoped that the girl was planning to place a bet using a large wad of cash that she had rifled from under her father's mattress, say, money was money, and he was currently in no position to turn down a bet, regardless of the size.

'Okay, sunshine, you give me that coin, and if French Fancy comes first in the next race, I will give you ten of them in return. How does that sound?'

To Noni, that seemed extremely reasonable, so the pair struck a deal. Off she went to find a good spot to cheer on this French Fancy fellow—and support is what the horse desperately needed, seeing as the thoroughbred hadn't won a race in over a year, as the bookmaker knew only too well. Feeling extremely pious, given the day that was in it, Noni thought that aside from giving her vocal cords a good workout, there would be no harm in having a little word with her new friend, Jesus. Firstly, she thanked Him for allowing her to eat some of His delicious body earlier in the day, and while she didn't want to be too demanding, she asked if it would be possible for Him to help her horse, French Fancy, run as quickly as her best friend Tommy O'Toole, who was, by and far, the fastest person she knew.

'If he wins, I promise that I will always do my homework, and I'll never smoke one of Daddy's cigarettes again.'

As soon as she had finished her prayer, the race commenced. Noni didn't know what she was looking at; she was only treated to a brief glimpse of the horses before they disappeared around the corner. Behind her, people roared at the top of their voices—not in the way Mrs Ledwidge did when someone misbehaved in class; no, their cries were more reminiscent of how her father listened to a football match on the radio or when he spent 'grown-up time' with Mammy in their bedroom.

Noni found the furore infectious, and the next thing she knew, she was being taken over by some outside force, clambering onto the railings and cheering louder than anybody else around her. She felt her belly was about to burst; her cheeks were on the verge of flames!

'French Fancy, French Fancy, French Fancy!' she repeatedly screamed with complete abandon.

Some of the other punters took Noni's lead and jumped up

onto the railings—Navan Racecourse had rarely witnessed such excitement! For the third time since the race began, Noni caught sight of the horses, but she didn't know which one was her sweet French Fancy, so she decided to shower them all with love, hoping that a dollop would land on the right one.

The horses were now on the home straight, and Noni could see that three of these mighty steeds were neck and neck; whether French Fancy was amongst them was yet to be determined. As if her little life depended on it, Noni let out an almighty roar that was so powerful, she, with her dainty communion dress, fell off the railings, landing on the muddy ground with a thud. And with that, the race was over.

Ill-prepared for an accident to stand in the way of her new pinafore, Noni jumped to her feet and pleaded with those around her to reveal the winner.

'French Fancy, that's who bloody won,' replied someone, almost on the verge of tears.

Noni couldn't believe her ears: her darling horse had risen to the challenge and won! She was going to get her pinafore after all! It was the most extraordinary feeling in the entire world, one that Noni would spend the rest of her life trying, unsuccessfully, to replicate.

After she had collected her winnings, Noni proudly marched over to her father to tell him of her success. Not knowing whether to be proud or ashamed, Mr Duggan bent down and held his daughter's cherubim face in his hands.

'Noni, promise me that you will never, ever do that again. Gambling is the worst vice there is, and it will destroy your life.'

Given the ecstasy of what had just occurred, Noni couldn't understand why her father would say such a thing. The past fifteen minutes had been the best of her life, and, in a few days, she would be the proud owner of a beautiful, red pinafore. But it seemed easier to agree with her father than try to make him see sense, so Noni sweetly told him that she would never do it again.

Forty years later, Noni, now Sister Fidelma, only wished that she had kept her word as the woman lived nothing short of a double life. By day, she was one of the most committed and devout members of the Order of Saint Aloysius; by night, she was a hardened criminal, struggling to pay off the mushrooming debts that she had accumulated due to her gambling addiction. Stolen from the convent, Sister Fidelma had recently flogged jewel-encrusted crosses, gold-coated chalices, precious artwork and historic bibles to dubious pawn dealers who, conveniently, never asked any questions.

But the money she received for the loot wasn't enough to satiate one particularly unscrupulous loan shark, Dennis, who demanded to be repaid the entire ten thousand euro she owed before the end of the week. (On a whim, his Russian girlfriend had decided she wanted a patio just in time for barbeque season, and bricks and mortar didn't come free—although Dennis did know a hardware store in Robinstown where he could easily pinch them, so maybe they could. Even still, he wanted his money back!)

Sister Fidelma had no choice but to borrow the convent's debit card and pilfer its funds. Besides, she had just been given a sure-fire tip, so the nun would soon be well-positioned to repay both the convent and Dennis – and no one would be the wiser. The plan was bulletproof. Except for one thing: she discovered that the card had suddenly vanished.

Later that afternoon, which was the same day that Sister Agatha had set off on her travels, card in hand, it was Sister Fidelma's turn to take some of the elderly nuns on a drive to Townley Hall, a beautiful, wooded park on the border of Counties Meath and Louth. Given their vintage, exercise and fresh air were of the utmost importance to the nuns. Sister Fidelma was so distracted by Dennis' threat that she failed to notice that the convent's oldest residence wasn't on board the mini-bus.

What's more, during the afternoon stroll, Sister Fidelma, who had only one ear in reality, misheard a conversation that sinus-suffering Sister Imelda had gone to support a grieving cousin following a misjudged haircut. Later that evening, when the alarm was raised that Sister Agatha was missing, Sister Fidelma informed the Mother Superior that there was no need to panic as the Dustbin had simply gone to visit a relative for a while.

Under normal circumstances, the Mother Superior might have questioned this claim following a good night's sleep, seeing as Sister Agatha didn't have any relatives—in mourning or otherwise. Instead, she spent the day assisting Gardaí to ascertain which hooligan had smashed the chapel's stained-glass windows. Whoever the culprit (it was, of course, Dennis, giving Sister Fidelma a final warning), the Mother Superior concluded that they must also have been responsible for plundering the convent's most coveted possessions—such as their collection of crosses, chalices, artwork and bibles. If she had noticed that the Debit Card had also vanished, along with a healthy portion of the convent's savings, she would probably have blamed the same hooligan.

Superintendent O'Shea had suspicions that both the vandalism and theft were the work of a gang of youths who had been terrorising Navan of late—or the Meath Mafia, as they had been recently christened. For the time being, the dubious deeds of Dennis, Sister Fidelma, and, most importantly, Sister Agatha went unnoticed.

FIVE

Seeing as Ravishing Rita was so accommodating in Dublin Airport, Sister Agatha wondered if lightning might strike twice today. After arriving at the Tunis-Carthage International Airport, she made a beeline for the Information Desk. This time, she was no better than poor Wayne, almost breaking out into a sweat while conversing with the young assistant behind the counter. Gifted with the most beautiful almond-shaped brown eyes she had ever seen, Sister Agatha believed that should Wassim, as his name badge indicated, uproot to the Emerald Isle, Jean-Pierre would be forced to up his game to prevent Rita from falling for this man's beguiling charms.

'You have two options,' he advised, his smooth voice reminding her of the delicious chocolate ganache Sister Josephine once made for Christmas. 'As there's only one train going from Tunis to Kebili, and it left two hours ago, you can either wait until the next one tomorrow morning –'

'Or?'

'Or you can join the Sahara Explorer tour right this minute, which will bring you to some of our country's most beautiful attractions along the way.'

'I see. And at what time will that option have me in Kebili, dear?' she quizzed, trying, unsuccessfully, to emulate his dulcet tones.

'It won't be until tomorrow afternoon either, I'm afraid.'

North Africa had always enchanted Sister Agatha. As a teenager, when she left Kilberry to pursue her vocation as a nun, her parents had bought her a collection of books to mark the occasion. (Knowing their daughter to have a curious and active mind, they had been concerned that the Holy Bible might prove repetitive after a while.) One was a splendid picture book that showcased exotic destinations from around the world, and even though photography had its limitations at that time, the young postulant acquired a wonderful sense of countries like Tunisia. With its vast Mediterranean coastline, soaring Atlas Mountains, unique salt pans and the sublime Sahara Desert, she thought it seemed only enchanting!

Yes, Sister Agatha was losing a day in her ambitious quest—a day she didn't have to spare—but the old gal decided to make lemonade out of lemons, which was particularly apt, as her host country was ripe with the fruit.

'Where do I sign up?'

Should the rest of Tunisia prove half as pleasant as this brief exchange with the dashing Wassim, Sister Agatha was sure that her short trip to North Africa's smallest country would prove to be quite memorable. She was also certain that the champagne from earlier hadn't properly worn off.

* * *

Initially, Georgina McGregor thought the absolute world of her son, Dougie. The journalist made it her business to show off her pride and joy to every last person she met in her hometown of Glasgow. Whether it was for the benefit of her local butcher or florist, the baby—and his shock of blonde hair—was paraded in front of them as if he were the Second Coming.

Since her beloved husband passed away a month after Dougie's arrival, Mrs McGregor was heartbroken. The only thing that kept her from following in her late partner's footsteps was her devotion to her darling son. In Dougie, she could see the man whom she had married when she was just nineteen years old: his eyes, his hair, his smile, his spirit. In Dougie, her husband lived. Few would deny her such extreme bragging rights; after her loss, her excessive love for the wee child was only natural.

As the years passed, their co-dependent relationship became a little Greek. When Dougie turned thirteen and his body started to shapeshift, the teenager should have been allocated his own bedroom, seeing as their large house in Glasgow's leafy suburbs boasted not two but three of them—and all en suite, at that. Instead, the unlikely couple continued to share a bed, just as they had done since Mrs McGregor first brought him home from the hospital.

One afternoon, Dougie's school was forced to close because of an infestation of deadly false widow spiders (ironic, given what would soon happen). He found himself unexpectedly home alone, idle. Sprawled across the bed, he started rifling through a collection of his mother's magazines and stumbled across a fashion catalogue. Even though he wasn't holding out too much hope that the latest budget-friendly fashion trends for women were going to be too entertaining, he decided to flick through its pages nonetheless—that was the level of his boredom!

As he reached the final section, little did he expect to fall upon a whole anthology of scantily clad women, all happily modelling the latest underwear, bikinis and negligée without a care in the world! Suddenly, the young teenager started to experience feelings that were entirely new for him—and they weren't entirely unpleasant either. Rather promptly, he followed the example of the ladies who smiled up at him from the magazine and removed most of his clothes. Without being overly analytical about the situation, the thirteen-year-old explored his body with the same zeal that the Spanish explored the New World – a subject he should have been learning about that day in school.

But before he could properly alight at his final destination, as it were, he heard the sound of his mother's heavy footsteps ascending the stairs. With the speed in which scurvy spread in Columbus' ships, the lad threw on his clothes. The very moment he returned the unsoiled magazine to its rightful place, his mother waltzed in, thankfully none the wiser. Dougie sat cross-legged on the edge of the bed as he stuttered through his account of the day's dramatic school events.

'I have a proposal, Mummy,' Dougie mentioned the following morning over breakfast. 'What would you think about amending our living arrangements?'

Even though she'd feared this conversation for some time, Mrs McGregor's heart sank at the suggestion. She was convinced that moving rooms was the first step in her son's plans to abandon her. Ill-prepared to lose her one true love for the second time, she decided to take action. Finding inspiration in her beastly editor, Mr Hamish—a dictatorial slave driver who had achieved absolute control by stripping his staff of self-worth—Mrs McGregor stopped showering her only child with praise and affection. Instead, she initiated a campaign of terror—criticising and jeering him at every turn.

'You're putting on weight!'

'If we had the money, I'd send you for elocution lessons!'

'Remind me tae get you some new soap; the other stuff obviously doesn't work!'

Knowing that Dougie had a sensitive disposition, just like his late father, Mrs McGregor was delighted that her barbed comments had the desired effect and cut straight through him. One day, he was the debating team captain and showed much promise as a footballer and athlete; the next, he was an awkward loner who wouldn't say boo to a goose. He waved goodbye to his independence and instead surrendered to his highly dysfunctional relationship with his tyrannical mother. If someone ever told Dougie that it would be the world's fifth-oldest person—a nun, at that—who would ultimately assist him in cutting those toxic apron strings while on a spring break to Tunisia, he would have laughed in their face.

Except, when the chance meeting took place, the now fifty-two-year-old had utterly forgotten how to do such a thing.

* * *

Mehdi, the young and sweet-natured tour guide, stood at the top of the bus beside Firas, the remarkably gruff driver. Even though there were only three passengers present—Sister Agatha, Mrs McGregor and her son, Dougie—he had been using a microphone throughout the expedition. (It later emerged that twenty Americans had cancelled due to a bout of salmonella. Seeing as Mehdi had gone to great expense to rent the equipment, he was determined to make use of the nifty device.)

'We are soon approaching our first stop,' Mehdi informed the trio, almost deafening them in the process, 'the beautiful Amphitheatre of El Djem.'

'Will ye ever put away that stupid microphone once and for all, ye fool!' Mrs McGregor, at the end of her rope, roared— embarrassing not just Mehdi but also her son, and not for the first or last time during their holiday.

Sister Agatha was unbothered by the sound of Mehdi's little toy as Sister Imelda's violent snoring had given her years of experience dealing with noise pollution. Armed with thick cotton buds in each ear, she happily nodded and smiled, and as she spotted their first—and rather magnificent—destination in the distance, she congratulated herself for having the wisdom to take this tour. (She also made a mental note to thank Tayri for residing in such a spellbinding country—before sending her skywards, of course.)

Before they stepped off the bus, Sister Agatha spotted Mrs McGregor surreptitiously removing a bottle of water from her son's bag. She concealed it under her jacket, which she then left on her seat.

'Right, let's see what the fuss is about,' she screeched, pushing past her son. 'Old Jim—is that what ye said the amphitheatre was called, Mehdi?'

Sister Agatha instinctively disliked her new travel companion and could sense trouble brewing ahead. As the group walked towards the stunning, ancient site, the supercentenarian was most responsive to the heat. It was an experience she had rarely enjoyed before, having spent her entire life in Ireland—the land of not just a hundred thousand welcomes but also a hundred thousand raindrops. Mrs McGregor, meanwhile, was not so enamoured with the warm conditions and dramatically fanned herself with the collection of handwritten notes she had grabbed from Medhi's hand. Sister Agatha became increasingly aware that her Scottish counterpart possessed a delicate constitution and had little interest in keeping these grievances to herself.

'Jesus H. Christ, the heat! And it's only March!'

Built by the Romans and often incorrectly described as a colosseum, the Amphitheatre of El Djem was, according to Mehdi, the third biggest in the world and possibly the last one built in the Empire. It may have been constructed during the third century, but it remained immaculately preserved, leaving Sister Agatha captivated. She couldn't help thinking about how genuinely talented God's children were. (Of course, sometimes, He got it wrong, with the taxing Mrs McGregor being one such example.)

As the group made its way up onto one of the upper tiers, Sister Agatha looked towards the basement area where, in the cells, the gladiators and wild animals were housed before combat. She could almost imagine the crowd of thirty-five thousand spectators salivating at the mouth as those bloody battles unfolded many moons ago. While she hadn't properly worked out the exact method by which her first victim would meet her grisly end, she thought employing the services of creatures as brutal as lions, wolves or wild boars would be unnecessary—and, logistically, a nightmare to coordinate.

It turned out that it was a modern-day duel taking place right beside Sister Agatha that was now demanding most of her attention. It appeared that Dougie had forgotten to bring his mother's bottle of water with him, and now the claws were out.

'D'ya want me tae die from dehydration or something?' she probed while swatting him on his bare leg with her walking stick.

Sister Agatha wasn't sure what Dougie's answer was, but the Irish nun leaned towards a yes. Despite what she had seen on the bus earlier, Sister Agatha had no desire to become embroiled in a family dispute. She decided to keep her own counsel even when the excursion, which she had been thoroughly enjoying, ended abruptly.

'There's always one who ruins everything, amn't I right, Sister?' Mrs McGregor barked.

'Indeed,' the one-hundred-and-eighteen-year-old tartly replied.

As they were frog-marched back to the bus, Sister Agatha was annoyed that she still hadn't received an opportunity to make use of the disposable camera she'd picked up along the way—it wasn't every day you received a chance to travel the length and breadth of the world, and she was determined to document as much as possible. Before they made their way onto the vehicle, Dougie turned to Sister Agatha and mouthed an apology, which she reciprocated with a friendly, reassuring smile. Having endured numerous crabby Mother Superiors over the years, she knew what it was like to be at the receiving end of such unfair vilification. Onboard, unsurprisingly, Dougie could not find the water, leading to an embarrassment of apologies. Beatifically, his mother accepted his contrition on the assurance that such carelessness wouldn't happen again.

'The patience of a saint, that is what I have!' she humbly acknowledged.

Once on the road again, she discreetly reached for the missing bottle from under her jacket and guzzled the contents whole, a sight seen by Sister Agatha alone. While Mrs McGregor wasn't on the assassin's original hit-list of four, should the browbeater keep up these shifty shenanigans, she soon would be.

SIX

When Dougie had reached the age of eighteen, Mrs McGregor finally conceded that it was time for her son to have a room of his own, safe in the knowledge that five years of oppression had provided the most satisfactory results. Her now lumbering son was going nowhere, that much she knew. While the damage to his spirit was almost irreversible, Dougie's new quarters lightened his heavy heart. Not only did he paper the four walls with posters and photographs from the *Star Wars* films, but he also kitted out his bed with Princess Leah bed linen and placed a host of memorabilia on a shelf above the pillow. On the first night in his new bedroom, the sleep he enjoyed was, by and far, his best yet. But his dreams soon turned into a nightmare when he woke up to find his own, real-life Darth Vader furiously destroying all his prized tributes to Jabba the Hut and chums.

'They're a fire hazard!' his mother screamed, tearing down the posters in a scene that could have fit nicely into a sequel of *Mommy Dearest*.

Dougie leapt out of bed and begged his mother to stop. After all, some of the things she was wrecking were worth a week's wage!

'Mummy, please be careful,' he begged. 'Actually, why don't you go downstairs and get some breakfast—I'll take the rest of these things down?'

But his pleas fell on deaf ears.

'Get into the bath this second. Your aunt is expecting ye at nine o'clock—her roses are in dire need of a good pruning!'

Admitting defeat, the young man limped into the bathroom and readied himself for a day taming his aunt's overgrown garden.

As the water flowed from the taps, he wished he had a real lightsaber and not the plastic ones his mother was smashing—how he would put it to good use! He removed his (*Star Wars*-inspired) pyjamas, took a deep breath, closed his eyes, and submerged himself in the water.

When he surfaced again, his mother towered over him.

'Scoot over, I've worked up a right sweat after all that redecorating.'

Over the next twenty minutes, Dougie and his mother sat in the bath together without a single word being spoken.

* * *

Sister Agatha was enjoying a siesta when Mehdi asked if anyone was a fan of *Star Wars*—though without the assistance of a microphone this time, thanks to a certain Narky Knickers. Even if she were awake, it was unlikely that Sister Agatha would have understood the cultural reference – or possibly misinterpreted it as some long-running feud between Hollywood celebrities, similar to the fisticuffs between Bette Davis and Joan Crawford, say. (The present Mother Superior was a die-hard fan of *Whatever Happened to Baby Jane?*, a film that she repeatedly insisted the sisters watch during Cinema Sunday.)

Dougie, on the other hand, was wide-awake and even more so upon hearing the mention of his favourite film. His loud and animated 'Yes!' irritated his mother and woke Sister Agatha.

'You're in for a surprise!' Mehdi continued.

Not wanting to appear rude, Dougie decided against revealing to his host that he was well aware that the next stop on the itinerary was Matmata and that he had been counting down the minutes until their visit there. The village consisted of a cluster of cave-dwelling homes; their distinctiveness inspired filmmaker George Lucas—so much so that Matmata featured in two of the blockbuster movies. Months earlier, when his mother had suggested forsaking their annual trip to the Costa del Sol and making a trek to Tunisia instead, he couldn't believe his ears! At that moment, all those decades of relentless cruelty faded away.

Seeing how excited her new friend seemed, Sister Agatha smiled. If anyone deserved a little happiness, it was that poor lad.

When the bus turned into the car park, Dougie was set to explode! He double-checked that he had his camera (as well as his mother's damned water) and rushed towards the bus door.

It wasn't just Dougie who was relishing the moment, although for another, more sinister reason. Mrs McGregor had treated herself to a haircut the winter previously when she read a travel feature in a magazine documenting Tunisia's breath-taking beauty. It also highlighted that any *Star Wars* fan would be in their element on account of the otherworldly Matmata. Knowing that her son lived for the films, she concocted a little plan: it wasn't just her recently coloured hair that had a streak, after all.

'Me angina is playing up on me again,' Mrs McGregor now shouted at Mehdi at the top of her voice.

Dougie stopped cold.

'Carry on to the hotel, will ye, Faris, or else you'll be bringing me tae the nearest hospital!'

The confused driver looked at Mehdi, who in turn looked towards Mrs McGregor's crestfallen son to get his thoughts on the matter. Dougie had always been convinced that the morning when his mother destroyed his *Star Wars* collectables could never be matched in terms of heartache, but he was wrong. Reluctantly, he nodded to Firas to continue to the hotel.

Mrs McGregor, who didn't know where her angina was even if it had been giving her trouble, sat back, delighted at how perfectly the plan she had been hatching for four months had played out.

* * *

The gang was booked into the Sahara Star for the night. Sprawling, exotic and vibrant, the hotel was the complete antithesis of Sister Agatha's meagre digs in Ireland—much to her delight. With over a hundred rooms and five suites to call its own, the establishment was, according to the manager who welcomed them on arrival, 'a haven of luxury and elegance, bathed in softly filtered light'—a description the Navan nun didn't quite follow, but she had a suspicion that should this dashing man and his mellifluous voice recite the telephone book, it would have sounded only glorious.

As he ushered them through the reception area, which

dripped with chandeliers and popped with turquoise tiling, the manager babbled on—albeit poetically—about how the hotel was renowned for its 'refined hospitality' and 'sensuous ambience'. Sister Agatha, taking photographs of her surroundings, wanted to send a postcard to the convent at home, detailing the magic of her new surroundings – she could only imagine their envy! (Although, she also suspected that such emotions would turn to anger after realising they were footing the bill.)

The manager eventually bade farewell and allowed two porters to escort the guests to the second floor, where their bedrooms awaited.

'See you at dinner, Sister,' Dougie muttered, almost inaudibly— hardly surprising, the nun thought, seeing as his ogre of a mother had long since stolen his voice.

She entered her quarters for the duration of her short stay at the hotel. Crossing the threshold, Sister Agatha gasped, convinced that Doctor McManus had killed her after all and that she had now arrived in Heaven. She was so bowled over, the old gal couldn't even muster the words to thank the porter properly.

'It's... Thank... I don't....'

'No need to thank me,' he said before revealing that the Americans, forced to pull out of the trip at the last minute, were actually due gratitude. Because of their sensitive dispositions, they were left bedbound in Tunis, meaning that she and her tour group were given the best rooms.

'And to think of all the criticism salmonella has previously faced,' she joked, although her efforts were met with a blank face.

Alone, she slowly explored her new residence, savouring every moment. With its white marble floors, red velvet wallpaper and king-sized poster bed, it was the most luxurious space in which Sister Agatha had ever set foot – and sure to rival the interiors of the Sistine Chapel. The candy-coloured en-suite—with its Jacuzzi bath, two sinks (two!) and tower of fluffy, cotton towels that almost kissed the ceiling—was so spotless that she dared not disturb a thing. But, out on the balcony lay the *pièce de resistance*: when she looked down, an adorable courtyard, peppered with palm trees, terracotta benches, and a central ornamental fountain, greeted her; when she looked up, a million dazzling stars filled the night's sky—and all of them appeared to be winking at her alone.

At that moment, this Irish lass felt like Queen Agatha of the Sahara—and how she wished that her reign would never end.

That evening, after feasting on some delicious *kosksi bil ghalmi* (or lamb couscous, as her waiter explained), Sister Agatha decided to skip the evening entertainment by the pool. Instead, she thought it best to return to her bedroom, concerned that the spicy food would make a reappearance. (The earlier incident in Charles de Gaulle Airport was more than enough for any lady to endure in one day.) More importantly, she had yet to hatch a plan for the following morning's main event: the killing of Tayri Chakchouk.

She reminded herself that this holiday was a working one, no matter how much she would enjoy the scheduled magic show or all-male band (their ponytails and paisley shirts portended to an entertaining evening).

There is no time for conviviality!

Sister Agatha knew that her first target lived in a mud hut just a few miles from where her hotel stood. Even though the nun believed that there was no time like the present, she felt that this oft-used idiom was trumped by the one that praised preparation as being key. And seeing as she had been too preoccupied with merely reaching her destination—not to mention being distracted by the many jewels that Tunisia possessed—she hadn't had sufficient time to investigate the most efficient way of ending another person's life.

Back in her bedroom, she wrapped herself in a bathrobe and took the pencil and pad from the bedside locker to jot down some possibilities.

They think of everything here, she praised while admiring the luxurious texture of the paper. On the verge of brainstorming, the sound of the band outside was proving too inviting—they were even playing Don McLean's 'Vincent', her favourite song!—so, to remain focused on the task at hand, she needed to block out all temptation. With steely determination, Sister Agatha marched over to the balcony to close the doors—as she did, she spotted Dougie sitting alone in the courtyard, staring straight ahead of him, deep in thought. He cut a lone figure and greatly contrasted with the similarly aged men nearby who were having the time of their lives, dancing or enjoying a cheeky nightcap.

There had been moments during the day when Sister Agatha could see the dying embers of a fire struggling to stay alight in Dougie's eyes, which was a good sign—at least they hadn't been extinguished for good. He may be at the beck and call of a certain despot, but she was sure there was still hope for him. What's more, Sister Agatha was fond of him, convinced that he would make the loveliest husband for someone—as soon as he escaped from his mother's ever-tightening claws. She removed the rosary beads from underneath her habit and held the emerald tightly.

'Does this dysfunctional mother-and-son relationship remind you of anyone, dear heart?' she whispered. 'Your mammy might have won a hundred years ago, but I'll be damned if history will repeat itself – not on my watch!'

Yes, just like Sister Anna-Maria, who, since childhood, had longed to jump into a swimming pool, but fear prevented her from doing so, a little encouragement was all that was needed for a successful outcome. Sister Agatha decided that tomorrow would not only be about ending one person's life, but it would also be about helping another start theirs. After all, if Sister Anna-Maria could swim across the Irish Sea at the ripe age of sixty-five, anything was possible.

The very instant that Sister Agatha returned to her bed, she fell backwards and into a deep slumber. And who could blame her? Being such a philanthropic do-gooder was tiring work, after all.

SEVEN

The following morning, an obliging waiter drew Sister Agatha a map to Tayri's house. It seemed the one-hundred-and-twenty-year-old enjoyed celebrity status, and the Irish nun wasn't the first person who wanted to visit her. In the end, the plan itself unfolded with much ease—at least the initial part. Sister Agatha would travel with the others to the nearby oasis, where everyone would enjoy camel rides. From there, she would give her guide a few *dinars* to stray briefly from the main group and detour to Tayri's humble abode (so long as he was of the brown-envelope persuasion).

What happened after that remained to be seen, but Sister Agatha knew that she would have to act swiftly to succeed. After all, her guide would be waiting outside the hut—regardless of how willing he ended up being, Sister Agatha suspected that he wouldn't be too supportive of the killing of someone as revered as Tayri Chakchouk.

'Good morning, everyone,' a breezy Mehdi said, boarding the bus. 'I hope you all enjoyed a good night's sleep because we have a busy day ahead of us, isn't that right, Firas?'

Firas might have been an asset to the tour operator because of his fine motoring skills, but he was about as engaging as a bell pepper when it came to his people skills. As such, he didn't even attempt to reply.

'Now, before we set off,' Mehdi continued, undeterred, 'I have a little suggestion that I would like your opinion on. What would you think about a little restructuring of the day's itinerary?'

Sister Agatha bolted upright—this wasn't the sort of talk she wanted to hear.

'I know someone was left a little disappointed yesterday because we didn't manage to visit Matmata,' he acknowledged, leading Mrs McGregor to release a long, dramatic sigh.

'I hope ye never have tae contend with angina,' she shot back.

'Of course, it was nobody's fault,' Mehdi added, trying to be as diplomatic as possible, 'but there might be a way to fix the problem.'

'What is it you're suggesting?' a worried Sister Agatha probed; was her innovative plan about to fall apart at the first hurdle?

'As magnificent as it is, the visit to the Salt Lake of Chott El Jerid never requires the full two hours we allocate for it. So, if we take some of that time, have lunch on the go, and skip visiting the carpet factory (they're extremely overpriced anyway), I think we should just about have enough time to return to Matmata for a brief walkabout. What do you say?'

Dougie closed his eyes and held his breath.

'All these changes are taking place after the camel rides, am I right?' Sister Agatha asked.

'Exactly.'

'Then, it's fine with me!'

Tears of joy lined Dougie's eyes. Was it possible that all of his prayers were, at long last, going to be answered? He turned to his mother, his face filled with hope and longing. Mrs McGregor stared out the window, giving the impression that she was considering the proposition when, instead, she was savouring every minute of her son's agony.

'I appreciate your kind offer, Mehdi; I do,' she finally responded, 'but I think it's best if we stick tae the plan, as arranged.'

'But—'

'That's me final word, Mehdi. Dougie, apologise tae the group for being so troublesome.'

'He wasn't—' Sister Agatha interjected.

'Say you're sorry, son!'

Following an uncomfortable silence, her fifty-two-year-old son bowed his head and mumbled an apology.

'Louder and clearer!' Mrs McGregor barked.

'I'm sorry, everybody.'

'That's better. Now, are we going tae get a move on? I can hardly wait for that camel ride we've been promised.'

Admitting defeat, Mehdi nodded to Firas, who turned on the engine—with that, their road trip continued as planned.

Sister Agatha looked towards Mrs McGregor, who happily relaxed in her seat—a smug, self-satisfied smile now etched across her face. The one-hundred-and-eighteen-year-old was left wondering if maybe she could kill two birds with one stone today.

* * *

The evening before, the trio had received nothing more than a taste of the Sahara Desert; it had been far too dark to appreciate its immensity and splendour fully. Today, they were in for a treat. Stretching the whole breadth of Africa, from the Atlantic Ocean in the west to the Mediterranean and Red Sea in the east—and taking in ten countries along the way—the Sahara had no qualms about making its presence known. Like all those who had visited here before her, it was love at first sight for Sister Agatha. When she looked in one direction, the sand appeared golden; in another, brown; and in another, white. More than anything, she felt it had the appearance of an image in some children's storybook, almost a figment of the illustrator's imagination.

Wholly seduced by the sight before her, Sister Agatha was just short of crashing through the bus window, throwing off her sandals and racing across the never-ending expanse of dunes. But that would hardly be fair on poor Faris—he might not be the friendliest of chaps, but the curmudgeon didn't deserve to spend the afternoon in some shoddy garage getting the pane replaced, particularly seeing as the temperatures were whizzing past thirty degrees.

With its windows still intact, the bus soon pulled into a make-shift car park where a rickety shed stood somewhat apologetically in the middle. From the rumbling growls that Sister Agatha could hear, she assumed that her new mode of transport—and unwitting accessory to murder—waited within. Mehdi assisted his three charges from the bus before leading them towards the man who appeared to be supervising proceedings. Sister Agatha noticed that his shoulders were broad, indicating someone dependable and trustworthy—and not the typical characteristics of a crooked accomplice. Fortunately, his duty was limited to collecting money, and soon she was allocated one of his employees as her guide. He was a young man whose thin body required a good feeding—something that costs money —something that Sister Agatha was prepared to offer in return for his assistance.

Perfect.

The guide handed her a white barracan robe, along with a headscarf. She was delighted with the costume change, especially as this new attire would afford her an air of anonymity later in the morning—an elderly lady in a nun's habit fleeing from a murder scene might give the game away, she feared. The camels, complete with their single humps, finally made their much-anticipated appearance and Sister Agatha, Dougie and Mrs McGregor were designated one each.

Synchronised, the three striking animals politely lowered their behinds to the sand to allow their passengers to mount them with ease. Sister Agatha refused to indulge in any trepidation—she was a farmer's girl, after all. Without assistance from her guide, she deftly perched herself on the camel's back, and as he stood upright again, she felt a marvellous sense of exhilaration. She had not been on top of an animal since her childhood days but felt completely at ease sitting behind the hump despite the long interval.

Speaking of humps, Mrs McGregor was currently in one as she was having the most terrible time mounting her camel. Sister Agatha enjoyed watching the tyrant show a little vulnerability for a change. Those glimpses of fragility were fleeting, and rather than endure the embarrassment any further, Mrs McGregor decided to forego the ride.

'Sod this, I'm going for a tipple instead,' she announced before heading towards a nearby café for wine. She was about to demand her son accompany her, but he was already perched proudly on top of his camel—and on the move, much to her annoyance.

'He'll pay for this later', she mumbled to herself, disappearing up some dusty road.

Sister Agatha wasted no time either and followed closely behind Dougie.

'Isn't it only mind-blowing, Sister?' he exclaimed, his enthusiasm infectious.

Sister Agatha nodded, and while the vista was undoubtedly magnificent, it paled in comparison to Dougie's remarkable transformation. Even in this brief moment out of his tormentor's shadow, he seemed taller, more vital. For the first time, he looked alive.

'It most definitely is, dear heart,' she replied, immediately realising that the poor chap had to go it alone—and the only way to make this happen was to give him (or the animal on which he sat) a good old-fashioned kick up the bottom.

Sometimes, it's the only language people understand, she told herself while preparing for her first daring deed of the day. Taking advantage of the fact that her guide was distracted swatting a mosquito away from his face, Sister Agatha grabbed the whip from his hand. Battling through the pain her arthritis caused, she lashed the derrière of Dougie's camel with all her might! The stunned animal released a long, loud groan before darting across the desert; Dougie, utterly bewildered by this sudden and abrupt turn of events, grabbed the grips and held onto them for dear life!

It is said that, on sand, a camel can beat a horse in a race, and the impressive speed in which that particular one went—even with a middle-aged chap on his back—only endorsed that claim. The faces of the two guides filled with horror (how would they explain this to their broad-shouldered boss?), and they bravely dashed after them on foot, even though they both knew it was a fruitless endeavour.

Alone, Sister Agatha cheered Dougie on, which she did with the same level of enthusiasm Sister Fidelma had shown all those years ago when cheering on French Fancy at Navan Racecourse.

'Go and have an adventure!' Sister Agatha shouted after him, thrilled that she was now no longer obliged to murder his mother.

While the power of the sun prevented her from watching Dougie disappear into the distance, she heard him celebrating, full-voiced. If those deep, guttural sounds he released received a translation, they might have said: 'Free at long last!'

After the initial euphoria of Dougie's emancipation had passed, Sister Agatha was forced to revise her plan. In liberating her vexed and miserable Scottish friend, she had suffered some collateral damage in that she'd also lost her guide. Thankfully, this fearless explorer was equipped with dogged determination as well as her hand-drawn map, and the kind waiter at the Sahara Star assured her that Tayri's hut was only a hop, skip and a jump away from the car park.

'I can handle this myself,' Sister Agatha confidently declared before she and her camel sallied forth.

She was grateful for the temporary peace as it afforded her time to contemplate her strategy for Tayri's murder. She was prepared to have blood on her hands but only in the figurative sense, so she decided not to concern herself with anything as crude as stabbing or shooting. Questioning whether she had the energy for strangulation, the Irish nun admitted that she did not. Even though she refused to indulge her arthritis, Sister Agatha was the first to acknowledge that anything deviating from basic movements, such as lifting a bag or dressing, would be an ordeal. While toying with the idea of using one of Tayri's medical instruments as a weapon, she worried that this might deprive others of some life-saving elixir if it broke in the scuffle. Her options were running out…

Seeing as she shared a name with the maestro of crime fiction, Sister Agatha scolded herself for her inadequacy. If only she had been able to finish reading *Murder on the Orient Express*, she would probably be teeming with ideas. However, a two-day thunderstorm in the mid-thirties had resulted in the convent suffering a leaking roof. The blasted deluge of rain that made its way through the cracks had damaged, amongst other things, their extensive Agatha Christie book collection. Rather than berating herself for the books she hadn't read, she decided to focus instead on those she had—notably, the Bible. If ever a text existed that documented the whole gamut of gruesome murders, it was the scriptures:

Jesus' crucifixion; Cain and Abel; Herod and John the Baptist; Judith and Holofernes; Noah's Ark; Sodom and Gomorrah. As she scanned through the pages in her mind, she thought that it was, in places, no better than some top-shelf Penny Dreadful!

Just as she started making a shortlist of possibilities ('Would it be excessive to serve Tayri's head on a platter?'), the nun, suddenly lightheaded, noticed something strange in the distance. While her eyesight had certainly passed its glory days, with the help of her tinted glasses, she could make out Dougie in the far distance, returning towards her! Except, it seemed as if he had now disposed of his camel and replaced it with an enormous elephant! What's more, he was surrounded by a tribe of nomadic people who enthusiastically played a range of stringed and percussion instruments.

What a fantastic transformation!

On the verge of indulging in some self-praising for assisting this metamorphosis, Sister Agatha realised that the scene in front of her was nothing more than a mirage. Moments later, her eyes battened down, and she slumped forward on the camel. A barracan and headscarf—on top of a habit and veil—in thirty-five degrees heat would prove a little too overwhelming for most people, particularly if that person was a one-hundred-and-eighteen-year-old travelling outside of her home country for the first time in her long life.

EIGHT

Illi was only ten years old, but she could play football better than any adult in Fatnassa – including her older brothers, who had long since given up attempting to get the ball off her. She may have been too young to appreciate her hero Zinedine Zidane at his zenith but still believed the French midfielder was the perfect ambassador for her fellow Berber people—infamous head-butts aside. She vowed to follow in his well-travelled footsteps and would, one day, lift the World Cup trophy.

When she wasn't practising her favourite sport, Illi threw herself into her schoolwork. With a good education under her belt, she hoped to gain employment in Tunis - and living there would allow her to impress scouts in the major football clubs. Along with her native language, Illi spoke fluent French, English and Spanish. If that weren't enough, her English was on a par with any native, something that proved extremely useful when the girl happened upon an elderly woman, drooped over a wandering camel, unconscious and in desperate need of medical attention.

Illi cut her football practice short and led the unexpected visitor to the home of her great-great-grandmother nearby. She, of all people, would know how best to rejuvenate this poor traveller; after all, Illi's great-great-grandmother had a remedy for everything, having been around for so many years.

In fact, she was the fourth oldest person in the world.

* * *

A kaleidoscope of colours greeted Sister Agatha when she finally awoke. Around her, sparkling fabrics, which hung from a central wooden beam, adorned the large space. An array of cushions and rugs lay strewn across the floor. Disorientated but overwhelmed by the sight in front of her, the nun now wondered if Doctor McManus' original week's prognosis had been optimistic and questioned if she had already transitioned from one world to the next.

'Ah, you're awake,' a young girl gently said. 'Here, have some more of this—it will give you strength.'

Gently, she lifted Sister Agatha's head and placed a glass on her lips filled with some potent drink. Even though the invalid's tastebuds were somewhat hostile to the experience, she instantly felt the colour return to her cheeks. Slowly, and with the help of her little guardian angel, she made her way to an upright position.

'You speak English, yes?'

Sister Agatha nodded. 'You might tell me who you are, my dear—and where I am?'

'My name is Illi, and you are lucky that I found you, or you might not be alive. It is dangerous to travel across the desert unless you are used to it.'

Before Sister Agatha could rustle up an excuse for doing such a silly thing, a voice sounded from behind them. Even if its owner were not surrounded by a wealth of ornate and decorative jars and decanters, Sister Agatha immediately knew that she was in the presence of health practitioner—and rival—Tayri Chakchouk. Granted, Sister Agatha was feeling dopey, and her eyesight remained blurry; even still, she thought that the recent image printed in Le Temps didn't do her hostess any justice. Tayri wore a striking mango and lime-coloured wrapper and sat on a wooden chair. Her face, free of any veils or headscarves, was delicate but immaculately preserved; the numerous lines it boasted were beautiful, triumphant and to be admired—a celebration of her long life.

Sister Agatha noticed brightly coloured stones lining the hut's base and wondered if they had a purpose other than decorative. Almost reading her mind, Tayri picked up one and handed it to the unexpected caller.

'Each stone represents a member of her family,' Illi explained.

'Her late husband, children, grandchildren, great-grandchildren, and great-great-grandchildren. There are one hundred and ninety-five in total.'

Sister Agatha thought it was a charming sentiment, and as she returned the amber stone to the lady of the house—or hut—Tayri shook her head and, in a soft, delicate voice, said something to her guest. (Unlike Illi, the one-hundred-and-twenty-year-old hadn't yet expanded her linguistic skills beyond her mother tongue.)

'She said that she wants you to keep it.'

'Oh, I couldn't possibly—'

'She insists. By taking the stone home with you, her family will be able to travel far and wide and see the world.'

Tayri smiled rather excitedly, making it impossible for Sister Agatha to refuse.

'Besides,' Illi continued in hushed tones, 'that particular stone represents my uncle Jamel, who disgraced our family by having a relationship with a married woman in America. Even worse, she was a politician. The farther away you take that stone from here, the better.'

Sister Agatha gave a say-no-more nod and placed it into her pocket. She then decided to test the medicine's effectiveness by getting to her feet, which she did with surprising ease.

Is it any wonder that Tayri has lived as long as she has, necking back a tumbler of those tonics each day, the nun mused.

Now fully revived, it was time to park such sentimental pleasantries and return to the pressing matter at hand: the killing of Tayri Chakchouk. Indeed, it was ungrateful to carry out an act on the very person who had just saved her skin but needs must, after all. With only a few more days to live, Sister Agatha didn't want a new pen-pal with whom she could exchange correspondences and reminisce about their chance encounter. No, it was too late in the day for such gaiety, even if Tayri was proving herself to be an exemplary hostess.

Just as Sister Agatha ransacked her mind for the most effective approach to take (stoning her to death with her one-hundred-and-ninety-five relatives would probably be a little vulgar and unnecessary), she spotted her camel recharging his own batteries at an oasis mere metres in front of Tayri's hut—a sight that left her having something of a Eureka moment. After spending the morning searching the dark recesses of her mind for the most suitable method, the answer came to her so quickly that Sister Agatha could hardly believe she hadn't thought of it sooner.

'I fear it's time to get back to my group; that's if they haven't already sent out a search party,' Sister Agatha calmly told Illi.

'I'm not sure if that's a good idea,' the young girl replied. 'It's almost afternoon, and it's only going to get hotter out there.'

'Now that I am refreshed, thanks to your great-great-grandmother's miracle remedy, I could travel to Egypt, I'm certain!' the nun assured her.

Not wanting to argue with her elders, Illi relented. 'If that's the case, I will accompany you.'

'You'll do no such thing,' was the firm response. 'You've both done more than enough. If it weren't too much trouble, though, it would be lovely if Tayri would accompany me to my camel outside.'

Tayri was long overdue her afternoon nap at that stage, exhausted having spent the past few days being interviewed by enthusiastic health bloggers, desperate to learn her medicinal secrets, but her exemplary hospitality forbade her from revealing as much. With help from Illi, she stood up and walked with her guest towards the oasis outside.

The plan had unravelled in Sister Agatha's mind instantaneously. At the edge of the oasis, the nun would succumb to the Saharan climate once again and faint. Her unfortunate stumble would see her 'accidentally' knocking over Tayri, who, in turn, would go headfirst into the oasis pool, never to surface again. Even though Sister Agatha was not one for tooting her own horn, she felt the plan was inspired! She couldn't resist breaking into a cheeky smile—if she had realised that this murdering lark was so easy (and so much fun!), she would have kick-started her career years ago. Some of the former—and challenging—Mother Superiors might have thought twice about how they ruled the roost if that were the case.

* * *

Before becoming a tour guide, Mehdi had different career ambitions: he wanted to be a pilot. After turning seventeen, his architect father received a job offer in Copenhagen. It was such a fantastic financial and professional opportunity, turning it down was never an option. The only problem was that young Mehdi had just been accepted into a prestigious pilot-training programme in Tunis, due to start at the end of the summer.

'I've dreamt about flying my entire life—how could you possibly stand in the way of that? You must let me stay!' Mehdi argued; his angular face was riven with anxiety.

As it turned out, there was little need for convincing; his parents were well aware that their eldest son was an aviation fanatic, obsessed with planes ever since his grandfather had gifted him a toy model when he was a toddler. How could they forget that every Sunday for almost fifteen years, Mehdi insisted on being brought to the airport to watch the many planes come and go, mesmerised? Of course, Mehdi was allowed to stay put.

Within a month, his parents and three younger siblings had gone northbound and Mehdi, having the house to himself, was the newly appointed king of the castle. Nonetheless, the freedom that the teenager—and soon-to-be-world's-best-pilot—had been afforded wasn't something he would take for granted; he refused to succumb to his friends' pressure to throw parties. While they were welcome to come over and share a few Celtia beers now and again, only his beloved girlfriend, Nadine, was invited to stay over. (Her parents were such heavy sleepers that an earthquake wouldn't have generated so much as a stir, so sneaking out of her house after dark was child's play for the girl.)

Two months passed, and Mehdi prepared himself for the first day of the rest of his life. The excitement was electric! The week before enrolment, the recruit was asked to undertake a medical examination, something Mehdi was sure that he would easily pass. Except, it emerged that he was colour-blind. When Mehdi opened the letter from the academy and read the words printed in black and white (or was it blue and white?), a hundred gunshots to the heart would have been less painful. Naturally, he called the admission office immediately, hoping that it was a mistake or prank. It wasn't. Unlike the planes that had always fascinated him, his lifelong dream to become a pilot wouldn't be taking off.

Unable to make sense of what had just happened rationally, Mehdi took every last plate, cup and glass from the cupboards and blasted them against the wall. Still unsatisfied, Mehdi opened his parents' drinks cabinet to smash its contents, but just as he was about to hurl a bottle of *boukha* through the window, he stopped: wouldn't it be more satisfying if he drank it instead?

And that was how Mehdi became an alcoholic of the non-functioning variety. Within months, he had dumped Nadine, put on three stone, and become an angry, bitter loner. The only person he interacted with was the man who sold him liquor at the local store. Simply put, to avoid a crash landing, Mehdi needed a parachute. Fast.

The lost soul was thrown a lifeline when his father's contract suddenly ended, and they returned unexpectedly to Tunis. After the initial shock of seeing their son's dramatic fall from grace, they started to implement a series of tough-love strategies, the most successful of which was the inspirational psychologist they introduced him to, and after a long, challenging year of healing, Mehdi was ready to return to the real world again.

Having finally accepted that flying wasn't meant for him, Mehdi focused on another aspect of travel and became a tour guide. Being on the move and surrounded by other people seemed the perfect antidote to his broken dreams—so long as everything ran smoothly and free from conflict.

When the news broke that two of his guests had disappeared into the Sahara Desert—one of them being close to a hundred if a day—Mehdi couldn't handle the situation and the inevitable fall-out. He ran to the bus and threw his rude colleague Faris out on his ear, who, in turn, landed on the group's one remaining guest—the horrid Mrs McGregor, flattening her with his many muscles. Mehdi ignored her cries for help, turned the ignition on and vanished across the dunes.

When Mrs McGregor was eventually rescued and managed to clear the sand from her mouth, ears and eyes, she was far from impressed to discover what had transpired that morning. It wasn't just Faris who sported one of the black eyes she dished out; it was every sinner who was unfortunate enough to cross her path that day.

* * *

Energised by the fact that she was on the verge of becoming the world's fourth oldest person, Sister Agatha, was taken aback by how sprightly she felt nearing the oasis. Thanks to her daily diet of exotic concoctions, Tayri didn't lag too far behind. As she attempted to focus on the task ahead, Illi, who had been so helpful earlier, now proved to be a burden. Proud that her great-great-grandmother had been alive across three centuries, the youngster was determined that Sister Agatha should know all about her many accomplishments.

'She once met Gandhi, Mother Teresa, Nelson Mandela and even Madonna!'

Not for the first time since leaving Navan, Sister Agatha had no choice but to insert her earplugs into their rightful place to quieten the roar of the young girl's relentless boasting. This section of the oasis consisted of two palm trees surrounded by what could best be described as a small pond—almost unworthy of hosting such a sensational event as a juicy murder, the nun felt. It was a good job Tayri was so petite; otherwise, the measly level of water would not have been sufficient for the enterprise.

The three finally arrived at the edge of the oasis. The young chatterbox continued to praise her great-great-grandmother to the high heavens (a place where Tayri would soon be visiting, all going well). Still, since Sister Agatha needed her senses to be sharp for the big moment, she reluctantly removed the buds from her ears. Now, she was busy trying to drown not only her rival but also the sound of this girl's endless soliloquy.

'Who would have thought that the baby born on 29 February 1896 would live to her current age—and meet so many famous people?' Illi continued.

Sister Agatha didn't even feign interest in what was being said—she was too preoccupied preparing for her big theatrical moment. She positioned herself behind her target, placed her hand on the emerald ring that dutifully remained in place under her habit and took a deep breath.

Lord, give me the strength to carry out this… somewhat questionable deed, she prayed. *There is no way back. It is my only option.*

But, as she concluded her private exchange with God, Sister Agatha made an

extraordinary realisation. She stopped cold.

What words did the little girl just utter?

Shocked and confused, she quickly turned to Illi. 'What did you say your great-great-grandmother's date of birth was?'

'29 February 1896,' the girl repeated, unable to conceal her pride.

Sister Agatha couldn't believe what she was hearing. How had nobody cottoned onto this before? How had nobody exposed this back-alley quack for the fraudster that she was? How dare she attempt to fool the world into believing that she was one-hundred-and-twenty when she had, in reality, just turned thirty!

Until now, Sister Agatha had always thought that leap years were an absolute nuisance; at that very moment, she was of the persuasion that they deserved a Nobel Prize for Peace, for they had just saved the life of the upstart standing next to her.

'I knew there was something about you that I didn't trust,' she brazenly said to Tayri, and while the exact meaning of her words mightn't have been fully understood, the sentiment came across loud and clear.

'Is there a problem?' Illi questioned.

'Dear child, as thanks for your warm welcome, I'll give you a free bit of advice—don't believe a single word that comes out of your great-great-grandmother's mouth. That's if she is your great-great-grandmother! Who's to know?'

'I'm not quite sure I understand….'

'To put it bluntly, my dear, in Ireland, she's what we would call a shyster, a phoney, a charlatan, a swindler! Trying to convince the masses that she is worthy of poetry and ballads when she's barely of legal age to have a drop of whiskey! How we have all been duped!'

But Sister Agatha was willing to put such grievances aside because just like that, she became the fourth-oldest person in the world and, better again, her law-abiding status remained intact— for now, at least!

'Wahoo!' she screamed at the top of her voice! 'Wahoo!'

Tayri and Illi wondered if their guest was having another heatstroke. But before they could return her to safer lodgings, Sister Agatha embraced Illi and her double-dealing relative with more kisses than a Mills and Boon novel. With a large grin etched across her face, the nun mounted her faithful (and well-watered) camel and set off to the airport, not forgetting to factor in a pit stop at some phone box along the way to bring *Le Temps*, Tayri Chakchouk's most avid supporter, up to speed on the duplicity.

'Thanks for everything!' Sister Agatha shouted, disappearing out of sight.

Illi's predictions about the afternoon's rising heat proved accurate, but a now unstoppable Sister Agatha had work to do and woe betide that blasted sun if it stood in her way once again.

* * *

March 2016

Dear Doctor Connery,

From Scotland to the Sahara, and what a journey! Doctor, you would be incredibly proud of how much I have grown since my arrival here in Tunisia; you could say that I am a new man! And would you believe it is all thanks to a nun and a camel!

You have always been encouraging me to take ownership of the various anxieties in my life; well, not only have I done that, but I have also taken ownership of my entire life!! For the first time, I am free and no longer living under my mother's shadow. (Yes, I can now finally name it: she is a tormentor, a bully!)

I am writing to tell you that I won't make our appointment next Friday, as arranged. As it turns out, I won't make any more of our Friday sessions because I am staying put here in the Sahara—my new spiritual home! And it is all thanks to a beautiful and courageous Irish nun—a guardian angel who left my life almost as soon as she entered it.

But don't worry, I am not alone. Would you believe I have met somebody, and we have fallen head over heels for each other! While some might think that she looks older than her years, she is just thirty (but has achieved so much in that short space of time, I can assure you—what an inspiration!).

It was fate that brought us together. After finally cutting those wretched apron strings and disappearing into the Sahara (with the help of Sister Agatha), I was kidnapped and taken hostage by a small gang of dastardly teenagers. As they discussed how best to siphon funds from my mother's bank account ('You're welcome to it!' I kept trying to tell them), a football came flying out of nowhere and hit the leader in the back of the head, knocking him out cold. Metres away, a young girl defiantly stood. When the ball rolled back in her direction, she skilfully picked it up again and disposed of the second and third gang members in the same manner. I have not seen anyone with such talent! The World Cup awaits her, that much I know!

Illi, my diminutive rescuer, then brought me to her thirty-year-old great-great-grandmother (only in the Sahara!). Doctor Connolly, let me tell you: my oft-bruised heart has never experienced anything like it before. I have heard so many people shout about it, but I always thought it would bypass me: that crazy little thing called love! But it has finally found me and—wait for it!—my darling Tayri Chakchouk and I are to be married! And guess where the Big Day is going to be? Matmata! We have just discussed dates and have decided on May the Fourth (be with you!!!). I am so happy; I feel that I could burst with joy!

I just hope that someday, I can help someone the way Sister Agatha has helped me. I will be forever indebted to her.

I trust all is well back in Glasgow. Have your new double-glazed windows been fitted yet?
Yours,

Dougie McGregor.

P.S: Forgive all the exclamation marks. Blame the abundance of happiness!!!

P.P.S: Needless to say, not a word to the dragon!!!

NINE

FOR IMMEDIATE RELEASE
Traffic Advisory Notice for Chicago's Saint Patrick's Day Downtown Parade

Top of the morning to ye, Chicago motorists! There'll be some traffic restrictions in place tomorrow, Saturday, 12 March, due to the annual Saint Patrick's Day parade and concert. Motorists should expect disruption along the route between 10.30 am and 1.30 pm, although it won't be anything to lose your head over, faith. Dancers, gymnasts and marching bands will make their way from Columbus Drive to Grant Park for a knee-slappin', foot-tappin' three hours.

Organizers also have an incredibly special Grand Marshal planned for this year. Even though he is a humble man, the jazz musician will be 'blowing his trumpet' at some stage during the day! If you haven't figured it out yet, here's another clue: he is America's oldest living person. Begorrah begosh!

For further information on Chicago City Council's Saint Patrick's Festival and other events around the city, visit potofgold.com.

* * *

To arrive at her second destination, Chicago, where she hoped to convince jazz musician Porter Williams to play his final note, Sister Agatha had to board a connection from London's Heathrow Airport. If the occasion had allowed for it, the now seasoned traveller would have taken herself into the city on the off-chance that she might catch a glimpse of Queen Elizabeth or,

78

better again, the lovely Prince William and Duchess of Cambridge. As she made her way through the busy airport, she thought of Sister Mary Eunice, a confessed Royal fanatic who had to be rushed to hospital after watching the beautiful couple marry a few years earlier. Sister Agatha felt that the whimsical nun, cursed with a stoop and pronounced limp, would spend the remainder of her days even more doubled-over than before, thanking the Lord above for such a sighting. (If their little children were with them, she would probably die on the spot!)

It remained to be seen whether the success that Sister Agatha had experienced in Tunisia was fleeting. As soon as she touched down on English soil, the world's newly crowned fourth oldest person was faced with something of an unforeseen pickle, and it was all to do with having (or not having) the correct security documentation to enter the USA. Two days earlier, her religious regalia had roused suspicions at Dublin Airport; she questioned how the dice would roll today—would it be a help or a hindrance?

A kind representative of the airline company, who had made her aware of the situation, now directed Sister Agatha to stand in a queue that dealt with such matters. Waiting for her turn, she prayed that whoever processed her case would be a kind soul, eager to do a good deed. From what she could see, eight officials were seated behind one long desk—a mixture of both men and women, young and old. She scrutinised their faces, examining who might be a friend and who might be a foe. One man seemed to be making a sport out of being unpleasant, having sent two tearful passengers packing in the short time that Sister Agatha had stood in line. His wiry hair reminded her of a toilet brush.

Anyone but Toilet Brush, anyone but Toilet Brush, she repeated, eyes closed.

When she opened them again, who was waving at her to approach? Toilet Brush. Sister Agatha slowly made her way over to him, exuding an air of beatitude.

'Good evening, my child,' she solemnly said before presenting her case to receive the fast-track authorisation needed to board a flight to Chicago.

'I see,' he acknowledged in a relatively neutral tone, leaving Sister Agatha unable to ascertain which way this exchange was heading. He then stared at her in an intense and disagreeable manner, leaving Sister Agatha to believe that Toilet Brush would do the opposite of what was traditionally expected of such a utensil—he would block, rather than block free, her passage. Except he didn't. In this instance, the nun's pietistic robes softened the heart of the God-fearing man, even managing to turn his grumpy frown upside down.

'We'll see you get sorted, Sister, don't worry,' he reassured her in a thick American drawl. 'Just help me fill out this form. What is the nature of your visit?'

But Sister Agatha's inability to tell Toilet Brush the exact purpose of her trip now threatened the successful issuing of the vital authorisation. While aware that it would be unacceptable to divulge her real intention, Sister Agatha was reluctant to lie.

I'll keep it vague, she decided before revealing that she was Chicago-bound to 'better herself'. Her response did not have the desired outcome. Toilet Brush suddenly became suspicious that the innocent-looking nun in front of him intended to seek employment in the Land of the Free, and that was a different ballgame altogether.

'And how do you intend to "better yourself", Sister?'

His prickly tone informed Sister Agatha that to keep her dream of fulfilling her vow alive, she must proceed with caution while also avoiding any falsehoods, if possible.

'By praying,' she eventually replied—a sincere response.

'If that's the case….'

And after a few moments of form-filling and box-ticking, Sister Agatha was on her way.

'Be sure to say one for my daughter,' Toilet Brush instructed the America-bound passenger as she headed towards the boarding area. 'She is about to join the army.'

If she's as gullible as her father, the young soldier will need as many prayers as possible, Sister Agatha concluded.

* * *

Flying high above the Atlantic Ocean that night, the Dustbin was famished; her grumbling stomach could easily have been mistaken for the plane's engine. Spotting the cabin crew handing out food, she salivated at the mouth.

At long last!

Not wanting to abuse the unwitting generosity of the Order of Saint Aloysius—and aware that funds weren't limitless—Sister Agatha had opted for an Economy seat on this Chicago-bound flight. When the air hostess presented her with a meal, the nun immediately regretted her prudence. An emaciated chicken breast sat apologetically on a plastic plate alongside a couple of orange-ish carrots and green-ish peas - not even her Saharan camel would have been impressed by these efforts.

'I don't think I'll be eating this schlop, dear,' she told the air hostess, deciding that abstinence was more appealing. For the first time in her incredibly long life, the always-hungry nun turned down a dinner - how the sisters at home would be gob-smacked!

Sister Agatha attempted to quieten her hunger pangs by reading the guidebook she had purchased while waiting at Heathrow Airport (after saying a few prayers for a young American trooper, as promised). She decided that there was no time like the present to familiarise herself with the city that housed the world's third-oldest person. The nun felt it fitting that Chicago had endured a long history of felonies, similar to what she was due to undertake. For instance, it was here, in America's third-largest city, that Al Capone had carried out his reign of terror about ninety years earlier. She was sure that such a legacy would only inspire her as she carried out her own carnage on arrival.

Next up was another one-hundred-and-twenty-year-old, who went by the name of Porter Williams. From one of the articles that Sister Agatha had come by, it seemed that he had once been a prominent jazz musician, having played with Louis Armstrong and Nat King Cole, amongst many other stars. And it appeared that the endless hours spent performing in smoky nightclubs and swigging Malort liquor hadn't knocked a bother out of him, as

Doctor McManus would have said. Having married three times, Porter's final wife was the only one who had borne him any children—twins—but today, he was the last surviving member of this quartet. Sister Agatha would soon rectify that.

How? was her next thought. According to the guidebook, Chicago was dubbed the Second City because a pesky fire in 1871 had burnt the place to a crisp—its current incarnation was the result of the makeover. This calamity was often blamed on a klutzy cow lacking in spatial awareness, which, rather appropriately, belonged to another Irish troublemaker called Catherine O'Leary. As Sister Agatha read those lines, she wondered whether history could repeat itself with a torrent of wandering flames ending Porter's frustratingly robust form. But, as Mrs O'Leary's cow would surely attest, fires spread, and Sister Agatha thought another cataclysmic event might prove to be one too many for the city to overcome.

The reading continued, and Sister Agatha became attached to the other moniker Chicago had acquired: the Windy City. While this term was originally a reference to the local full-of-hot-air politicians, it had since become an appropriate description of Chicago's breezy conditions. Wouldn't it be magic if a gust blew Porter from the top of one of the city's numerous high-rise buildings? According to the enlightening guidebook in her hands, Chicago's architects were credited as the creators of skyscrapers, so it seemed a rather suitable exit for its eldest son. But nature can be troublesome at the best of times, and even though it was mid-March, she worried that, like the chicken she had just turned her nose up at, that plan might also turn out badly.

Being dependent on the wind might prove overly ambitious, but Sister Agatha was reluctant to abandon the use of the city's skyscrapers altogether. The number of times she and her cohorts at the convent had cracked, broken or smashed glass only proved how fragile the material was. (As a matter of fact, her right hand still carried a scar from a recent incident when she had become embroiled in a disagreement between Sister Ursula and Sister Ingrid—lifelong enemies—as they were washing the dishes together. After breaking the glass, Sister Ursula then proceeded to break Sister Ingrid's nose.)

Satisfied that she had stumbled across the bare bones of a plan, Sister Agatha thought it best to mirror the passenger seated next to her and rest her eyes for a brief spell. After recharging the batteries, she would then delve into the nitty-gritty of the murder itself, such as how best to lure Porter to the venue and push him through one of the windows. It was another marvellous idea—she was sure of it!

As she started to doze off, the nun couldn't help but admire Al Capone for having the energy to carry out so many deadly deeds in such a short space of time. Without even completing one yet, she was pooped!

TEN

Still at war with a bout of jetlag, Sister Agatha shuffled through the lively O'Hare Airport in a haze and suddenly worried that she had taken the wrong flight and ended up back at home. All around her were Irish flags, not to mention posters of *Darby O'Gill and the Little People*, pots of gold, shamrocks and pints of Guinness. Maybe the flight had to turn around because of bad weather—or the pilot had forgotten to switch off his immersion or leave food out for the cat.

As soon as she earwigged into the various conversations around her and heard the distinctive American accents, Sister Agatha was reassured that she had, thankfully, arrived at her intended destination. When she noticed a lady's T-shirt that displayed an image of a mitre-wearing, crozier-holding man surrounded by a slither of unhappy snakes, the penny dropped for Sister Agatha: Saint Patrick's Day loomed on the horizon. (When she then spotted a banner that read 'Happy Saint Patty's Day', she thought the printer must have started their celebrations early as only a drunk person would make such a glaring mistake.)

Since overhearing Doctor McManus claim that she had one foot in the grave, Sister Agatha had only eyes on the prize, and feast days for patron saints were of little interest to her. She had previously been informed that this particular day had caught the world's imagination, but it wasn't until now that she realised to what degree. Emerging outside, the nun didn't know what to be more taken by—the skyscrapers soaring in the distance or the additional tributes to the Emerald Isle on the airport's façade, notably an eye-catching green lights display.

While it was still a few days shy of the seventeenth, a traffic notice on the window informed her that the parade was taking place today, Saturday. By all accounts, the festivities promised to be a tremendous lark—they even turned the river green! But Sister Agatha refused to get distracted by the occasion: her only interest was Porter Williams and how best to ensure that this would be the last festival he would ever celebrate.

With her energy finally returning, the new arrival didn't think twice about skipping the long queue for the cabs, promptly hopping into the next available vehicle. No apologies were made for her transgression—not that anyone was asking for one. After all, the one-hundred-and-eighteen-year-old had long since cottoned on to the fact that few would deny an elderly nun some special attention. And if it aided her in completing her ambitious quest to become the oldest person in the world in such a limited timeframe, she might as well use and abuse such chivalry.

Sister Agatha felt that her taxi driver was terribly friendly—full of ideas and suggestions about how best to make the most of her stay in the city (a ride on the Ferris wheel on Navy Pier sounded like a lark, for instance).

'Unfortunately, I am here for business, not pleasure,' Sister Agatha informed her, 'but should my busy schedule allow for it, I'll be sure to follow your lovely recommendations.'

'How long are you going to be with us, Sister?' she enquired—a question that the nun didn't have an answer to at that moment. Flights out of the city were ten-a-penny, so, ideally, she would be heading east once again before the *Six-One News*. However, if Porter was like that mischievous mouse who arrived unannounced at the convent last Christmas, getting her hands on the scamp might prove tricky.

'I don't suppose you know anything about Porter Williams, do you?' the nun asked casually.

'What a dude!' the driver exclaimed. 'Everyone knows about him!'

It turned out that, like Tayri, the nun's next target was quite the local celebrity, thanks to his extraordinary longevity and gift for melody. But since his beloved wife's passing, compounded by a body slowing down, Porter had made very few public appearances in recent times. Following numerous requests from the city council, he had surprisingly agreed to be the grand marshal for this year's Saint Patrick's Day Festival. According to the cab driver, this honorary role required him to sit on top of a horse-drawn carriage, which would be led through downtown Chicago in front of thousands of spectators. In a change to the traditional schedule, this year, there were additional plans to make a pit stop at the Jay Pritzker Pavilion, where Porter would perform for the first time in decades.

'There's life in the old guy still, Sister!'

Not for much longer, Sister Agatha hoped.

While she wasn't one to turn her nose up at a musical recital, particularly if it involved the expertise of someone as celebrated as Porter Williams, it was the later disclosure about the afternoon drinks—due to take place in the Willis Tower—that whetted Sister Agatha's appetite.

'It will be a party to remember!' the driver promised.

Sister Agatha recalled reading in her guidebook that this lofty skyscraper was once recognised as the world's tallest. The author had documented the new additions to its hundred-and-third floor in great detail: a handful of glass balconies that extended about four feet from the façade. Called The Ledge, Sister Agatha thought it sounded like a tremendous feat of engineering and the perfect setting for a murder.

'Of course, it will be a private affair,' the driver added. 'You'd want to have the luck of the Irish to bag an invite into that party.'

I don't know about being lucky, Sister Agatha thought, reflecting on Doctor McManus' bleak prognosis, *but I am Irish...*

Without even reaching the city centre, she had already established what had to be done: somehow, she would join the parade, then align herself with Porter Williams before accompanying him to that exclusive, sky-high event. There, the chap would come crashing down to earth with a bang and a wallop! Better again, this all could be accomplished in time to make the evening flight, meaning that there wouldn't be a need to spend a single dollar on hotels or food (although it would be nice if the Willis Towers provided some light refreshments).

How proud the convent would be of her frugality.

* * *

Before kicking off her mission two days earlier, Sister Agatha would have been described by those who knew her best as single-minded, tenacious and focused. On the other hand, luck was not something she, or others, would have associated with her. For instance, the one-hundred-and-eighteen-year-old was yet to win the Christmas raffle at the convent. She also waited to be victorious at the Community Hall's Tuesday Night Bingo Bonanza, despite having played there every week since Year Dot. And, to this very day, every Hallowe'en had passed without her ever uncovering the ring in the barmbrack. (Although, when Sister Concepta had found it some months earlier, she realised too late and spent the night in A&E after it had become lodged in her throat. Therefore, the jury remained undecided on whether a ring-less status counted as being lucky or not).

However, since reaching Dublin Airport two days earlier, Sister Agatha was surprised by her good fortune. Even during tricky moments, chance had always won out. Squashed in the middle of an excited crowd of onlookers on South Columbus Drive, she now looked towards Heaven and pleaded with all its residents for that streak to continue. In case they had been distracted earlier in the day and were not up-to-speed with what she required of them, Sister Agatha closed her eyes and carefully reminded them of her objective for the afternoon.

I need to cosy up to Porter Williams and join him for a post-show beverage on the hundred-and-third floor of the Willis Towers, then find some way of shoving him off the building, resulting in me becoming the world's third oldest person. Does that sound feasible?

It was undoubtedly an ambitious proposal, so she needed her celestial friends on her side. After re-opening her eyes, Sister Agatha wasn't expecting Moses to have parted the crowds to either side, thereby giving her a clear path to Porter, who, with the assistance of a couple of fine-looking steeds, was making his way towards her, but the poor gal thought she might receive some inspiration at the very least—no matter how small. Instead, what greeted her was an inebriated teenager, barely able to remain vertical—and in desperate need of a strong cup of coffee or, better again, her bed. But when a security team member lifted the girl over the barriers and onto the street—and in spitting distance of her target—an idea formed in Sister Agatha's mind.

If you can't beat them, join them!

Following her time in the Sahara Desert, Sister Agatha was a dab hand at collapsing, so, without delay, she flounced onto the ground with a dramatic flourish. She kept her head upright in fear of being mistaken for a large black rock that could be mounted to afford eager spectators a better view of the action. After several kicks to the legs, a charitable soul finally noticed the nun's plight. Whether it was Moses' doing or not, the swarm of people moved to either side of her, and a strong, uniformed woman lifted her over the barriers. Sister Agatha was now only metres away from her prey. Conscious that the security guard was duty-bound to summon an ambulance, the nun realised that even if she were to take her inspiration from that famed Phoenix and suddenly rise from the ashes, the guard would not let her out of her sight.

And that was when Lady Luck finally arrived at the scene. Just as the security guard was about to signal to the First Aid team to approach, her phone rang – her girlfriend had just gone into labour. Watching the guard vanish down the street, Sister Agatha's pain and anguish of never winning the Christmas raffle faded away.

She looked towards the parade directly in front of her. Leading it was Porter, happily sitting in an elaborate carriage wearing a green cloak, topped off with an ill-fitting, woollen hat. He appeared to be in his element, waving at the adoring crowds. On foot, a small contingency was trailing the famous Grand Marshal; their suited attire suggested to Sister Agatha that they were the mayor and other important officials.

Perfect company!

Bold as you like, the world's biggest chancer rose to her feet, dusted herself off, and fell in line with them. The ease with which she was accepted into the fold based on her recognisable get-up led Sister Agatha to contemplate branching out from being just a cold-blooded murderer and becoming a thief as well. Her invaluable guidebook had revealed that the Art Institute of Chicago Building, located near her present position, kept a watchful eye over celebrated works, including *Nighthawks* and *American Gothic*. If she were to swipe them, they could animate her dreary cell in the convent.

But any thoughts of robberies and interior design abruptly ended when a hand landed on her shoulder. She spun around; behind her was a stern-looking man who would be more at home in a boxing ring than in the middle of a Saint Patrick's Day celebration. When he removed his other hand from his pocket, it wasn't a pair of handcuffs that he held aloft, but a large clump of shamrocks.

'You don't seem to be wearing any, Sister—would you like some?'

'I most certainly would, my dear!'

Armed with a touch of her beloved Ireland, Sister Agatha marched forward, and while she may not have just received four-leaf clovers, she was one lucky gal, that much was certain.

A short time later, the parade made the scheduled diversion and marched through the multi-faceted Millennium Park. Sister Agatha, taking as many photographs as possible, thought the giant bean—or Cloud Gate, to give it its official title—was rather amusing. Sister Ursula had littered nearly every corner of the convent's recreational room with similar attempts of modern art. Granted, the sculpture now standing in front of her was infinitely more successful than some of her wayward friend's previous efforts. (Who could forget her controversial version of Michelangelo's *La Pietà*—unveiled during the much-anticipated visit from the Archbishop of Armagh, forcing the then Mother Superior to take to her bed for two full days?)

When the parade continued towards the Jay Pritzker Pavilion, Sister Agatha was sure that Sister Ursula would appreciate its bold and unique design. The bandshell's steel headdress was quite the feat—and not dissimilar to the white cornette veils that some of her counterparts wore in other countries. Once again, she dismissed the idea of sending her dear, artistic friend a postcard because it might give the game away, but Sister Agatha promised to provide her with a blow-by-blow account of her adventures – complete with photographs - should she return to Irish shores.

Just as the day's excitement began to catch up with her, Sister Agatha was relieved to discover that the parade was temporarily putting the brakes on proceedings. Porter was assisted from the carriage and led up onto the stage. Everyone else made their way into the large park in front of it. The official, who had earlier added shamrocks to her habit, invited Sister Agatha to take a front-row seat. Delighted to rest her tired feet for a brief moment, she gladly accepted, slumping down on one of the chairs—while keeping an eye on her mark to ensure that he didn't do anything to hinder her perfect plan.

The atmosphere reached fever pitch when Porter took centre-stage; after allowing a moment for the crowd to settle, the legendary musician took a trumpet to his mouth. What followed, Sister Agatha could only describe as magical. While the nun wasn't equipped with the vocabulary of those clever music critics in the newspapers, she loved the high notes, low notes, long notes, short notes, and every other note in between. For five minutes, the jazz virtuoso dismissed the unfortunate ramifications of age and cast a spell on the thousands of admirers who had now bundled into this sprawling outdoor venue.

At home, Sister Agatha had always relished the Sunday services that involved beautiful musical interludes from the local choir, but anything she had enjoyed in the past paled in comparison to this experience. She felt the trumpet was an extension of Porter, or, even better, they were one. Despite her tiredness, she tapped her feet and had a hankering to trip the light fantastic. She looked around, wondering if anyone else might share similar inclinations to transform the space into a makeshift dance hall. Unfortunately, everyone remained in situ, with a subdued bob of the head or clap of the hands being the extent of their merriment.

Not to worry, she thought, rising to her feet, *I'll do it alone.*

That she was the antithesis of Russian ballerina Anna Pavlova didn't prevent her from creating all sorts of outlandish shapes—and what a wonderful way to stretch her creaky body following so many hours ensconced on planes! While some of those seated around her struggled to refrain from laughing and pointing, others found her free spirit inspiring and jumped up to join Sister Agatha in the revelry. Porter Williams may have been making a splash on stage, but it seemed that it was now Sister Agatha who was the real star of the show. What's more, the old doll would be the first to admit that she was relishing every single moment of it.

* * *

It had been several years since Porter had performed in front of a crowd of this magnitude. It had also been quite some time since he had performed at all. Following the death of Vondra, his beloved wife, Porter, who was eighty-seven at the time, didn't have the appetite to play any longer. Despite protests from his long-serving manager, his vast collection of instruments sat idle in his basement studio, gathering dust. While public appearances were few and far between, his music and legacy lived on. His legion of fans quietly hoped that, someday, he would return to the stage, although as the years passed, it had become increasingly unlikely.

Then Porter became the victim of a nasty betrayal. It transpired that his butter-wouldn't-melt-in-the-mouth accountant had been helping himself to Porter's savings, and on a wet January morning, the one-time millionaire discovered that there wasn't a red cent left in his coffers. Faced with the prospect of losing the house he and Vondra had made a home—with nothing left to leave his many grandchildren and great-grandchildren—the performer had no other option but to return to the music scene.

Having turned down numerous invitations to be the Grand Marshal for the Saint Patrick's Day parade, Porter finally agreed. Reluctant to simply strut through the city in a ridiculous carriage, the one-hundred-and-twenty-year-old suggested incorporating a musical recital into the itinerary. This offer was music to the organisers' ears (as well as the ears of his manager—the fee tripled there and then!).

The week leading up to the event, doubts started to creep in. At Porter's age, having lungs that still functioned was an achievement; making demands other than breathing might prove ambitious—and even ungrateful. However, Porter knew that it was surely going to be his last opportunity to command the attention of an audience that size. As he stood on the stage today, in full flight, he was happier than he had been in years, aided by the sight of a nun who, as far as his limited eyesight could tell, was similar in age and dancing as if there were burning coals in her shoes.

Look at what you've been missing out on, kiddo! Porter joked to himself.

And by the looks of things, he wasn't the only one admiring this sprightly sister; a large band of fans had formed around her and were energetically spurring on the showgirl. Who was this beautiful soul, busy captivating all around her? Curious to a fault, Porter gestured toward security to bring her up on stage.

* * *

At first, Sister Agatha thought the two burly uniformed men intended on reprimanding her for being a health and safety hazard, but when she detected a couple of disarming smiles on their faces, the knots in her stomach untangled.

'Porter would love it if you would join him on stage,' one said, offering his hand.

Sister Agatha's little band of supporters clapped and nodded their heads in encouragement. Swept away by the occasion, the nun threw caution to the Windy City and allowed the security officers to lead her up the steps and onto the stage. Her arrival was met with a cacophony of cheering from the thousands now crammed into the park. As she caught a glimpse of a giant version of herself on the screens positioned on either side of the stage, she thought it ridiculous—yet fabulous at the same time! Porter gestured for her to join him.

'Ladies and gentlemen,' he shouted into the microphone. 'There's no doubt that this magical lady has a unique rhythm after watching her cut a rug, but I want to know, can she work her way around a trumpet just as well?'

Up until now, the extent of Sister Agatha's musical escapades had been limited to a bit of self-conscious tambourine playing during celebrations in the early nineties to commemorate the Order's three-hundredth anniversary. Her participation only occurred because the then Mother Superior had been adamant that everyone was involved in some shape or form. (On the other hand, Sister Veronica, the perfectionist choir conductor, spurned that maxim about taking part was what counted and insisted that the inept Sister Agatha mime playing the tambourine instead. In Sister Agatha's defence, the harsh winter they had experienced that year had infuriated her arthritis.)

Before she could even contemplate refusing the offer, Porter played a long bass note. He then handed the trumpet to his new buddy.

'Do you think you could repeat what I have just played, Sister?'

Whether she liked it or not, their unplanned duet had commenced. Reluctantly, she accepted the instrument but feared that she would drop it, such was its weight. Seeing her struggle, Porter gallantly helped. Sister Agatha refused to allow herself to be seduced by the charm of her new friend; if she did, it would make the act that she was due to carry out on top of that skyscraper next to impossible. She blew the trumpet, but the sound that emerged was similar to that made by an elephant—one in extreme pain at that.

'Here, let me show you again, Sister,' Porter laughed before demonstrating what was required to make a more sonically appealing note.

But as she was receiving her spontaneous music lesson, Sister Agatha suddenly stumbled upon a naughty idea.

What a fantastic weapon that trumpet would make!

Her busy mind started to whir. All she had to do, she reasoned, was lift the piece of equipment above Porter before swinging it across the back of his head. What's more, she was even warmed up following her dancing. Yes, it seemed like too good an opportunity to miss. Except for one thing: the eyes of the city were on her. In a matter of seconds, Sister Agatha could be another rung up the ladder in her quest to become the oldest person in the world, but if she were to pursue this course of action, she would soon find herself spending her remaining few days incarcerated in some God-forsaken hovel, with a bunch of gold-toothed, tattoo-covered convicts as her only company.

There would be nothing glorious about that, she discerned. No, I must bide my time and stick to my original plan.

The euphoria of being this revered musician's ingénue was now wearing wafer-thin. Without so much as a by-your-leave, she marched off the stage, refusing Porter's invite to attempt another, more favourable note. While the spotlight was certainly appealing, Sister Agatha knew deep down that she didn't have the temperament to be anyone's sidekick.

ELEVEN

Tunisian-born Jamel Chakchouk always had notions above his station. The strikingly handsome, vainglorious playboy wanted to live in a castle, but not one made of sand. His mobile phone was awash with personal images showcasing his impressive physique, while his head was filled with dreams and fantasies about being the leading man in some international reality show. Jamel's self-obsession meant that he was the source of constant mockery within his small community in the Sahara Desert, not that he paid much attention to their juvenile jeering.

One day, I'll have the last laugh, he reminded himself repeatedly.

On the morning of his twenty-fifth birthday, fed up with living life as 'a peasant', Jamel visited his great-grandmother, Tayri, who slept soundly, surrounded by almost two hundred colourful stones, each representing members of her extensive family. He kissed her forehead before fleeing his hometown for good. After spending a few months in various resorts along the coast, Jamel had soon gathered enough money to buy himself a one-way ticket to Chicago. He had collected the price of his fare not through hard work in bars or restaurants but by taking advantage of lonely – and wealthy – middle-aged tourists holidaying in the country. He would fill them with sweet nothings before emptying their bulging purses.

In Chicago, Jamel eventually found lodgings in Pilsen, a vibrant suburb popular with immigrants. Quickly settling in, American life was everything he imagined it would be: diverse, prosperous, and overflowing with opportunities and possibilities. Within weeks of his arrival, the confident go-getter met Lucy

Flood, an up-and-coming politician who was canvassing the area one evening. Surprisingly, he didn't want to take advantage of her. Here was a woman who was attractive, fearless and well on her way to fame and fortune. He thrived on the fact that she was also ruthlessly ambitious; in her, he had met his match. A passionate affair soon began between the pair.

Jamel occupied his time imagining himself with Lucy in the White House, decked out in the latest designer outfits, being photographed by Annie Leibovitz and appearing on the front cover of *Vanity Fair* or *Men's Health*. He didn't realise until much later that while he spent his day in cloud-cuckoo-land, Lucy spent hers with her husband and three children. Foolishly, Jamel believed the promising politician when she said she would leave her family. As it turned out, the opposite happened. On the advice of her party, who was hell-bent on selling her as the reliable family woman who recycled, loved animals and went to mass every Sunday, Lucy eventually called a halt on the couple's dangerous liaison, leaving poor Jamel heartbroken.

And hungry. Every day and every night, the once-lean head-turner feasted on triple portions of tajine and couscous—anything that reminded him of home. How he rued the day he ever left the desert but having revealed his plight to them one drunken night, Jamel quickly discovered that he was now no longer welcome there. His heart was not just broken; it was on the verge of an attack.

While he never lost his appetite, the inconsolable young man soon lost all dignity and self-respect and began his own campaign, stalking his former flame at every chance. Wherever Lucy was, the now whale-like Jamel usually loitered only metres away. In the end, the politician was forced to take out a restraining order against him ('What a shame, he used to be so attentive to my needs!' she told friends over lunch one afternoon).

But that piece of paper was as much use as a hill of beans because a man in love would put Isaac Newton to shame in terms of inventiveness. When the Saint Patrick's Day Festival arrived at Willis Tower, Jamel stood a short distance away from Lucy.

He had managed to convince the official photographer that her images would surely make the front pages of the papers if there were someone dressed in a quirky costume standing next to that old fogey, Porter Williams. The photographer thought the idea was juvenile, but she struggled with her self-esteem and could never say no to anyone, so eventually acquiesced.

And so, on the hundred-and-third floor of the famous skyscraper, an eclectic group gathered to toast the success of the day's events. The guest list included Grand Marshal Porter Williams; the agile dancer, Sister Agatha; the adulterous politician, Lucy Flood; the she-says-yes-to-everybody photographer, and around two hundred officials. Not to mention a giant, life-sized pot of gold who planned to do something shocking with the help of a gun.

* * *

The lift, or elevator, that Sister Agatha took to the hundred-and-third floor lasted only sixty seconds. Initially, she was grateful for its briskness, anxious to complete her task and board the evening flight to her next destination, but as soon as the altitude pressure became apparent, she felt queasy and annoyed that there weren't more sensitive means of travelling to those lofty heights.

In its former incarnation as the Sears Tower, this skyscraper was once the tallest in the world, she and the delegation were told as they made their way onto an impressive observation area called Skydeck. There, a few years earlier, three glass balconies, dubbed The Ledge, had been added, offering daredevil visitors the opportunity to look directly onto the street one-thousand-three-hundred-and-fifty-three feet below. Porter Williams was now bravely stepping onto one of those scary ledges to drink a pint of Guinness and toast Ireland and its adopted son, Saint Patrick.

'I hope you're not afraid of heights, Porter!' one of the officials teased.

'Dude, I think I might need more than one pint to calm the nerves,' the Grand Marshal replied, unaware that should Sister Agatha have her way, that second libation would be consumed at the Pearly Gates.

While she was no expert in engineering, Sister Agatha was confident those who were had used panes that would be more than able to withstand this slight trumpeter's weight. To achieve success, she felt that something hefty would be needed to stand alongside him as he enjoyed his final taste of stout—something bulky enough to shatter the glass beneath him and wipe him out once and for all. She dismissed her suggestion of pushing a chair or table out onto the glass box—neither would be adequate for what was needed. (And she was sure that rearranging the furniture in such a manner would be frowned upon, and she had no intention of abusing her host's hospitality.)

She then investigated the possibility of pretending that a deadly spider was on the loose, which might lead to a few faint-hearted cry-babies running for cover on The Ledge alongside Porter. Sister Agatha needed those participants to possess a significant build for this to work—and even though she had heard that Americans enjoyed their generous food portions, those around her appeared to be skin and bone. Except for one—a man who had truly embraced the spirit of the occasion by dressing up like a pot of gold. Sister Agatha thought it was quite the achievement that he had managed to fit into the elevator in the first place, such was his width.

Before she entertained the idea any further, Sister Agatha shook her head and slapped her wrist. While she needed to dispose of her rival Porter Williams, she wasn't too crazy about there being casualties of war—and by the looks of things, this hefty party-goer had enough problems to negotiate without having to contend with being dead as well.

No, I need to keep collateral damage to a minimum.

When she started to mull over other solutions to her predicament, the pot of gold suddenly announced to the entire floor that he had a gun in his possession and demanded that everyone pay attention. Sister Agatha thought that the organisers would be most disappointed that all the hard graft that had gone into making the day so successful would now be tarnished by this person's ill-timed act of terrorism.

* * *

Even though Porter had fought in two World Wars, an abject terror ransacked his face when Jamel stepped out onto The Ledge and placed the weapon on his temple. It was not due to being held at gunpoint but because he worried that the glass wasn't going to withstand the weight of this new, unexpected addition. Like many people when they reached a certain age, Porter had spent time wondering how he would finally die, but not even in his wildest dreams did he consider his exit would be like this.

As his accented captor shouted towards some Lucy person in the room and demanded that she leave her husband and return to him—'where you belong!'—Porter reflected on his life, grateful that he had experienced so much happiness over the years. While his first two wives had turned out to be somewhat disagreeable, it proved to be a case of third-time lucky when he had met Vondra. Yes, she had stolen his heart but had, in return, given him the most incredible gift imaginable—their daughters, Kadisha and Kiandra.

If he had any regrets, it was that he didn't spend enough time with the loves of his life when they were alive. Instead, his other passion, music, always came first; after they had all died, he realised how foolish he had been and spent each day since begging for one more chance. Every morning, he visited their graves. Every morning, he brought them flowers. Every morning, he talked to them but never played—he had done far too much of that when they were alive. He told them what he had eaten for breakfast, what the weather was like, what his plans were for the day—innocuous things that were rarely mentioned face-to-face. He told them that he loved them and counted down the days until they were reunited.

And as this madman continued to point the gun at his head (during which the glass admirably continued to keep them both aloft), Porter felt content for the first time in decades. Thanks to the generous fee from today's parade, he had successfully saved his house—his grandchildren's inheritance—from being sold off to his debtors. And, at long last, he was going to be able to tell

Vondra, Kadisha and Kiandra to their faces what he had enjoyed for breakfast that morning: a poached egg, a tumbler of orange juice (anything more was too acidic for his delicate stomach), a single slice of dry bread, as well as a handful of prunes to keep everything moving. Although, the fear that this crazed, roly-poly bloke was currently instilling in him had made those prunes somewhat unnecessary.

* * *

What the neighbours said was imperative to Pete Flood, an outlook he inherited from his parents. It was of the utmost importance that people saw his family in the best light possible: the successful lawyer wanted others to look up to the Floods and aspire to be like them. Whatever wickedness happened behind those picketed fences stayed behind those picketed fences.

His successful political wife, Lucy, was rarely home because of her work, so it was left to Pete to run a tight ship. When their eldest son, Pete Junior, had announced that he was gay, Pete responded by giving him a black eye. (He was seventeen—how could he possibly know, anyway?) The following morning, he dragged him to the parish priest, who then subjected Pete Junior to a four-hour, turn-away-from-sin rant, and the only possible way to bring the misery to an end was by promising that he would never act on such heinous urges. Pete Junior ran away that very evening.

'He's gone to join the army and serve his country,' Pete told Mr and Mrs Victors and all the other residents on the street. 'If he dies in combat, then it's God's will.'

Pete had always been aware that his wife of twenty years was a two-timing strumpet, but it only became an issue when one of her toy boys refused to accept that the affair was over and had subsequently become nothing short of a nuisance. Every evening, when Pete drew the curtains, he would see the sallow-skinned lothario sitting in his car outside, a pair of binoculars in hand.

Taking out a restraining order had only exacerbated matters, and Jamel, as it turned out he was called, continued to pursue his stalking endeavours with commendable zeal. He would ring the phone every few minutes and shout graphic obscenities. Clothes were stolen from the washing line and later returned, boasting stab marks and blood. As much as Pete was impressed by Jamel's commitment, this tomfoolery had gotten out of hand, and it had to end.

Pete knew that Jamel would find a way of being present at the Saint Patrick's Day celebrations in the Willis Tower, so along with a bunch of shamrocks attached to the lapel of his new Ralph Lauren jacket, the devoted husband and father placed a pistol into his pocket. As they would say in Ireland, the jig was well and truly up.

* * *

Sister Agatha watched as the scene played out. She was too long in the tooth to get frightened by such matters but certainly felt uncomfortable. The pot of gold was distressed, and it seemed that love was at the root of the problem, and love's name was Lucy. As he held the gun on poor Porter (who remained admirably composed, if somewhat reflective), the pot of gold detailed the various highs of his relationship with Lucy. It was a good job that there were no children present, as some of the anecdotes being shared were especially intimate. Lucy cautiously approached the pot of gold to diffuse the situation, imploring him to put the gun down and promising that everything would be okay.

'Will you leave that bastard of a husband of yours? Will you?'

'I will. I swear to you that I will, so long as you put the gun away.'

Her words resonated with the transgressor, and he slowly lowered the weapon. But before Lucy could step onto The Ledge, another gun triggered, and a series of shots followed—and a promise that Jamal would 'never get my wife!' Some of these bullets hit Jamel, although most missed their intended target completely.

It was said that The Ledge was able to hold four tons, but that figure hadn't factored in the glass being shattered by a Glock pistol at close range. As the crowd gasped in terror, Porter Williams and the elephantine pot of gold went crashing through it, falling an irremediable one-hundred-and-three floors.

Amidst the chaos, Sister Agatha stumbled to the ground, resulting in the yellow amber stone that Tayri Chakchouk had gifted her dropping to the floor. As the petrified crowd rushed to the elevators, the amber stone was kicked from right to left, eventually rolling its way out the shattered Ledge and landing slap-bang in the middle of the pot of gold on the ground below. Sister Agatha entered the Willis Towers as the fourth-oldest person in the world. With the assistance of a sordid love triangle and a gun-toting scorned husband, she left being the third.

TWELVE

You are cordially invited to celebrate the wedding of
Edyta Balinski and Pawel Dragon
at
Lazienki Park, Warsaw on
Sunday, 13 March 2016 at four o'clock

The couple requests that any gifts take the form of donations to the Warsaw War Memorial, of which Edyta's great-grandmother, Benedykta, is a patron. There will be maximum security on the day, and entrance to the venue shall only be permitted by the wristbands enclosed. The happy couple asks that guests bring their dancing shoes because music will be played until the early hours of the morning!

Istniejemy na tyle, na ile kochamyv (We exist only when we love).
* * *

Marie Curie, the two-time Nobel Prize winner, was born in Warsaw, Poland's capital city. After a nine-and-a-half-hour flight from Chicago, followed by a brisk taxi ride from the Chopin Airport, Sister Agatha finally arrived in the centre and hoped that she, too, could be as innovative as the great scientist when it came to dispatching Benedykta Balinski, the world's second-oldest person. The city's newest visitor was let out in front of the unpopular yet magnificent Palace of Culture and Sciences—an unwelcome gift from a certain Joseph Stalin and a glaring reminder of Soviet domination in the city.

The Order of Saint Aloysius had once received an unwanted

present from one of Navan's most ardent and devout churchgoers when a 1995 referendum was passed to allow unhappily married couples to divorce. The aggrieved spinster rocked up to the convent on a wet Wednesday morning and presented them with a handmade ornament made from hundreds of matchsticks crammed into a giant sponge. One matchstick had a speech bubble attached to its head, asking: 'Where's Daddy?' It had proven unpopular with everybody in the convent, apart from the short-sighted Sister Annunciata, who thought it was a hedgehog made by the sweet children in school. It was stored away in a cupboard and only brought out when the aforementioned parishioner called around. Looking up at the Palace of Culture and Sciences today, Sister Agatha thought it was unfortunate that the Polish people couldn't take a similar approach, she conceded, because few cupboards could conceal it on account of its size.

So far, Sister Agatha had successfully obtained information about her targets by simply asking the locals; it seemed that those over the age of a hundred were, rightly, considered royalty and their every move was recorded. Luckily, this approach had been successful when she had questioned Kacper, the friendly air steward who had taken such good care of her on the journey over. While giving her a second helping of *sernik*, a delicious Polish cheesecake that just melted in her mouth, he revealed that Benedykta Balinski was due to celebrate the marriage of her great-granddaughter to one of the country's most successful entrepreneurs, Pawel Dragon. The city was at a standstill, and the excitement was electric. The pair had erected an enormous marquee in the famous Lazienki Park, and anyone who was anyone would be there, including the nun's latest target.

On the one hand, Sister Agatha was delighted that she had established Benedykta's whereabouts. On the other, she had a hunch that the place would be swarming with security, keeping any unsavoriness at arm's length, and doubted whether she was equipped to overcome such obstacles.

Three days ago, you were the fifth-oldest person in the world, she reminded herself. *Today, you are the third. Do not underestimate your skills!*

After this pep talk, she marched over to a street vendor to nab herself a *zapiekanka*, a delicious sandwich complete with sautéed mushrooms, cheese and ketchup. Refuelled, Sister Agatha set off in the direction of the Lazienki Park by foot (last-minute airfares, even Economy seats, carried exorbitant price tags, so she now had to be mindful of every cent—or, as it were, every grosz). Besides, after the snack she had just devoured—and the feast that her darling Kacper had conjured up thousands of feet in the air—she was in desperate need of exercise. Sister Priscilla, one of the few recent recruits to the Order, had once informed everyone that the camera added ten pounds and seeing as Sister Agatha was soon to be the world's oldest person and in high demand with the world's media, she didn't want to let herself down by being rough around the edges.

No, if she were bestowed such a prestigious honour, the nun wanted to look the part, so off she set off to the wedding by foot, hoping to burn a few calories in the process.

Sister Agatha and her now-blistered feet hadn't anticipated Lazienki Park's size. Despite the pain, she conceded that the ample space was required to house all its magnificent palaces, theatres and temples—as well as its many towering monuments of luminaries such as Chopin, the city's most famous son. Sister Agatha hobbled past these striking architectural delights, full of admiration, before finally stumbling across the wedding marquee. As suspected, it was surrounded by tall railings and an army of muscly security guards, busy intimidating well-wishers. In the crowd, Sister Agatha thought she recognised a troupe of can-can dancers from her stop-over at Paris a few days previously, although she wouldn't be confident standing up in front of a judge and admitting the same.

She skulked behind one of the many large trees dotting the park and observed the situation from afar. Her options were limited. The guests—beautifully turned out with hats and fascinators—sported wristbands that were being scanned at the front entrance. Poland was amongst the world's largest suppliers of apples, and as Sister Agatha looked at the overflowing carts lined up outside the marquee, waiting to be brought in, she wished that she was a guest. Not only would it allow her to murder Benedykta Balinski, but it would also let her chomp down on one of those scrumptious delicious Gala Royals. Sister Agatha was a living testament to 'an apple a day keeps the doctor away'; sometimes, if she felt giddy, she would indulge and have two! Looking at them now, she wanted to dive into the carts and bathe in their deliciousness!

Then, an idea formed in her mind. As she worked out the sketchy details, she could see that the plan was flawed, but after four days of travelling the length and breadth of the world, it was the best she could come up with. It was just so ridiculous; it might work, especially if she approached it like ripping off a bandage: she just needed to close her eyes and do the deed!

Devil may care, Sister Agatha strolled over to a second tree close to the carts and waited for the workers to become distracted. The arrival of a group of well-known, scantily clad celebrities did the trick, and without giving too much thought to the shortcomings of this hare-brained idea, the nun took a deep breath, blessed herself and dived into the cart. Battling to conceal herself within, she cursed the length of her habit. Following a bit of to-ing and fro-ing, she felt confident that her entire body was now adequately covered beneath the apples. What followed was a seemingly eternal waiting game, made all the worse by the fact that she was trying—and struggling—to resist temptation and not devour her camouflage.

Moments later, she heard voices edging toward her. A group of men surrounded the cart, and, judging by their tone, they were not the friendliest lot. How and ever, she wasn't here in Warsaw to make new friends, so they could be as gruff as they liked so long as they played their part and brought her to where she needed to go. No sooner had that thought crossed her mind, the cart moved and, at long last, it was en route into the marquee where, should luck continue to be her ally, she would find the means to eradicate the woman standing in her way of becoming the second-oldest person in the world.

While spatial awareness wouldn't have been one of Sister Agatha's strongest points, she was sure that the journey to the marquee was short, yet it felt like the cart had been on the move for an age.

Maybe we're going in through another entrance, she reassured herself, trying to ignore the niggling doubt that something was amiss.

When the cart did stop, the stowaway breathed a (silent) sigh of relief. Any delight was premature - as it started moving again. This time, the cart mounted a ramp into what Sister Agatha suspected was not the marquee. When an engine sounded, she was sure it wasn't.

THIRTEEN

Before becoming one of Poland's most revered spies during the Second World War, Benedykta Balinski was a famous Olympic skier. If it weren't for a family tragedy that occurred before she was born, she might have represented another country entirely. Her father hailed from Annecy, a lakeside city in the southeast of France, but after his first wife died from complications following childbirth, the widower immediately began a courtship with their Polish nanny. Keen to start afresh, they upped sticks to Warsaw. Once married, the couple had their only child together, Benedykta.

While French was spoken at home, the mechanic's youngest daughter had loyalty to one country alone: Poland. When she later played a pivotal role in emancipating the war-torn nation from German occupation, it came as no surprise to anyone. Few were aware that their golden girl actually jumped horses in the latter part of the war.

It had started promisingly for Benedykta. After joining the intelligence services in 1939, the then forty-four-year-old had used her experience as a skier to escort various agents and resistance groups from Hungary into Poland by way of the chilly, snow-capped Tatra Mountains. One such agent, a rather stout and bearded Englishman, had been so impressed by her fearlessness— along with her fluent French and knowledge of motors and engines—that he invited her to join the Special Operations Executive in London. There, success followed, and Benedykta soon earned the distinction of being one of the first female agents to parachute into France.

The blonde-haired beauty wasted no time organising the

transportation of arms from Britain, which she then distributed amongst resistance members. Under the guise of an amateur archaeologist, she even managed to gather crucial geographical information for future landings. The Nazis were no match for the fearless Benedykta!

Five years later, things suddenly became complicated. Benedykta received instructions to attend a party at the Gestapo Headquarters in the French capital and seduce the womanising chief, Herr Freudenberger, before extracting some vital information from him. Except, one small problem emerged: they instantly fell head over heels in love. Despite having an adoring husband at home in Warsaw, she began a passionate affair with the Nazi.

The honeymoon period ended abruptly one late summer evening. While walking by the River Seine, the couple was set upon by a freedom fighter named Olivier Guinot. Ill-prepared to allow her new German lover to be killed, Benedykta tackled this Nazi-hating *jeune homme*, killing him with her bare hands. A lifetime on the slopes set a person up for any task.

Weeks later, on 2 September 1945, her French associate accidentally learned of Benedykta's indiscretions with Herr Freudenberger, along with the brutal murder of Oliver Guinot, after discovering some of their romantic correspondences in a tattered envelope. Shocked by the revelations, he imprisoned the Polish traitor in his apartment's spare bedroom. Hours later, Benedykta took full advantage of the fact that her captor was inebriated, celebrating the end of the war, and strangled him before escaping back to Poland without anyone the wiser about how she had really spent the previous months in Paris.

With Herr Freudenberger cemetery-bound, Benedykta thought the best way to distract her broken heart—and ensure nobody started digging too deeply into her Parisian pursuits—was to ski. Three years later, she placed third in the 1948 Winter Olympics held in St Moritz, making her the oldest athlete to achieve such a victory.

Life soon returned to normal for Benedykta. She disappeared from the public eye but was certainly not forgotten—particularly in times of political uncertainty when the war heroine was wheeled out in front of the country to remind the Polish people of the importance of remaining loyal and patriotic to the motherland. In recent years, she had passed the spotlight onto her darling great-granddaughter, Edyta, a regular fixture on the social scene, who sent the country into a frenzy after aligning herself with one of the wealthiest entrepreneurs in Eastern Europe. Frustratingly, as Benedykta helped the twenty-one-year-old prepare for her big day, it emerged that her past had finally caught up with her.

After years of extensive and expensive detective work, a Parisian family had finally discovered that Benedykta was the person responsible for killing their beloved father and grandfather, Olivier Guinot, before dumping his body into the Seine. Her scarf, which had fallen to the ground during the attack, proved key in solving the case. They wanted retribution, but rather than going through the official channels to get justice, these blood-thirsty avengers thought it would be more satisfying to take the law into their hands instead.

When Benedykta learned that her life was in peril, she immediately created a network of moles around the city, who promised to give her the heads-up when a threat to her life emerged. After learning that the elderly nun who had enquired about her on a flight into the city was now, comically, concealing herself in an apple cart, Benedykta ordered her minions to bring the uninvited guest to the city-centre house that she was helping renovate for the happy couple. Benedykta was yet to pick out carpets or wallpapers for the various rooms, so nobody would be too upset if some blood were shed here or there.

* * *

It wasn't just Copenhagen that had a vested interest in bare-chested, long-tailed water sirens; the mermaid was also a symbol of Warsaw and given pride of place on the city's coat of arms. Sister Agatha could make out one such figure in the centre of a busy, medieval square outside the house. She had been sitting in a dark room for an hour with her arms and feet tied to the wooden chair, mouth gagged.

Earlier, when the truck had finally stopped, Sister Agatha prayed that she and the apple cart were being transported to some mart after the wedding organisers realised that they had been overly enthusiastic when ordering the fruit for Edyta and Pawel's big day. (Although, was there such a thing as too many apples?) If that were the case, Sister Agatha then anticipated the sight of an ageing nun hidden within the produce would cause jaws to drop, so she readied herself to take full advantage of their confusion and flee quick smart. Except, the truck's destination had not been a mart but the backyard of some empty, four-story house.

She now breathed deeply through her nostrils. To escape from this prison, she would have to quit her pity-partying and, instead, utilise some of the skills she was renowned for: her practicality, determination and single-mindedness. Before she could explore any possible means of liberation, the door suddenly flung open. Much to her surprise, it wasn't some rowdy ruffian who could make grown men cry; before her stood an old friend.

'Kacper?' she said after he ungagged her.

It was evident from his cheerless expression that he wasn't here to serve her a second slice of yummy *sernik*.

* * *

Kacper Zaleski was always in a rush. Even when he had nowhere to go, he felt it best to get there as quickly as possible. Such unnecessary haste might be traced back to his premature birth, having arrived a full three months before his due date—much to the embarrassment of his mother, who had been browsing the frozen food aisle in the supermarket when her waters suddenly broke.

Kacper's speedy approach to life ultimately proved to be his undoing. The day following his fortieth birthday, he had been driving to work. Even though Wlochy, where the Warsaw Chopin Airport stood, was a bustling town, the air steward didn't even consider slowing down. Having never been in an accident before, he wasn't sure what to make of the loud thud he heard while careening into the car park reserved for Polish Airlines staff. If he had hit an animal, the birthday boy wouldn't have bothered stopping, but he feared that he might have done some damage to his brand-new car—a gift from his wife—and if it had so much as a scratch, there would have been hell to pay.

But he hadn't bumped into a cat or dog; he had hit a child. As the boy lay sprawled out on the side of the road, all that Kacper could see in front of him was a life incarcerated in some godforsaken prison. His wife would be sure to take the keys back from him if that were the case. An elderly woman, wearing a shawl and sunglasses, tended to the unconscious boy. Spotting Kacper, she dragged him away from the scene of the crime.

'Meet me outside the Tomb of the Unknown Soldier tomorrow morning at ten o'clock,' she instructed. 'Now, get out of here before the *policja* come.'

And with that, Kacper fled, thanking his lucky stars for allowing such a discreet and considerate elderly lady to be present at the scene. It appeared that he wouldn't have to part with his new wheels after all.

The Tomb of the Unknown Soldier was a stately monument in the centre of Warsaw, dedicated to the nameless men and women who had given their lives for their country. Lit by an eternal flame, it was a popular meeting point amongst locals thanks to its convenient location. Kacper, always ahead of time, wondered how the exchange with his elderly guardian angel would play out. Seeing as his wages at the airport were modest at best, he hoped that she wasn't expecting remuneration for her silence. Maybe he could offer to do a spot of gardening or help her with the shopping, although they would need to establish some boundaries; otherwise, she might take advantage of his generosity. He didn't have to wait much longer to discover his fate because as soon as the hourly change-of-guard took place, he felt a light tap on the shoulder.

'Walk with me,' the elderly woman ordered in a low, calm tone.

As they strolled across the square, she informed him that while her grandson's condition had been precarious the night before, he would be fine—music to Kacper's ears! She now needed a favour. The woman's life was in danger, she revealed. There were constant threats to her life, and she needed protection. Kacper's gut told him that this woman was out for lunch, but he decided to indulge her, almost out of curiosity.

'How can I protect you?'

The woman advised Kasper that she needed him and his colleagues at Polish Airlines to be her eyes and ears, flagging any passenger inquiring about her. While her ramblings amused him initially (and, of course, he was extremely grateful that she was otherwise tight-lipped), Kasper was a busy man and had places to be, so he decided to end the bizarre exchange. Just as he turned on his heels, he noticed that the old woman wasn't alone; two burly men walked threateningly in their shadow behind them.

'Don't worry about that pair,' she said. 'They won't harm you so long as you do as I ask.'

On second thoughts, Kacper decided it might be best to give this possibly-not-so-batty lady his undivided attention after all. Besides, it wasn't as if her requirements were too demanding. He and his colleagues at Polish Airlines were naturally curious and continuously engaged with those who travelled on their flights, asking them about their plans in Warsaw, where they were staying and what they planned to do. Her request was simply an extension of that.

'Okay, that all seems straightforward,' he told her. 'I think we have a deal.'

Kacper held his hand out to shake on what they had agreed upon, but instead of accepting it, she grabbed him by the arm and wrenched him towards her with unexpected force.

'If you and your friends don't do as I demand, I will march down to the *policja*. I suspect they will be interested in seeing some footage that I managed to film from yesterday's accident,' she warned, revealing a camera in her hand.

Kacper assured her that he didn't want anyone knowing about the mishap from the night before, so he swore that he would do as instructed.

'What is your name?' he asked, just as the pair parted ways.

'Benedykta Balinski.'

When Kacper had time to reflect on the previous twenty-four hours properly, he thought he had won the lottery, falling into an allegiance with Benedykta. (Her name sounded familiar, but being on the go all his life, he had little time for national, patriotic figures). The outcome for knocking over a child due to speeding could have been much worse than having to keep a lookout for unsavoury figures who may or may not be on board his flights. What he hadn't realised was that he had been hoodwinked. The poor lifeless boy on the road didn't have so much as a scratch— or if he did, he didn't feel it because the unconscious victim was nothing more than a dummy.

Benedykta's frail body was slowing down, but the threats on her life were not. She had spent the evening before the incident with Kacper, fighting off a third knife-wielding relative of Oliver Guinot. Those aggrieved French sleuths may have been able to work their way around a magnifying glass, but they were clueless when it came to handling a machete. They quickly found themselves being reunited with the late Oliver much sooner than they had anticipated.

Benedykta had, once again, come away from the encounter unscathed, but she wasn't sure if this would remain the case. On top of her newly acquired bodyguards, she needed to establish a citywide network that could protect her – and those connected with the transport industry would be particularly useful. So, a blackmailing scheme was born where drivers were convinced that they had knocked down a helpless child, and to keep Benedykta— the only witness—quiet, they became her eyes and ears. Once in the fold, she would then get them to run the occasional errand for her, including the odd kidnapping or two.

Kacper was the thirteenth such chump Benedykta had drafted into her clique, a number that would prove extremely unlucky for someone who was of the persuasion that, since leaving Navan, fortune had been on her side.

* * *

Given the circumstances, Sister Agatha ought to have been a little concerned about the situation, but Kacper, who kept circling her while checking his watch, seemed so out of his comfort zone that she had to dig deep not to laugh in his face. He certainly appeared more at home serving delicious food or selling perfume thousands of feet in the air than playing the role of a hardened criminal.

Soon, a third person entered the room and the temperature suddenly cooled. Sister Agatha instinctively knew that the new arrival was more competent than the slithery air steward who had been so deceptively pleasant to her that morning.

'I hope I have not kept you waiting too long,' said a voice almost as creaky as the floorboards. 'You see, my great-granddaughter is getting married this afternoon, and it wasn't too easy for me to slip away.'

Benedykta Balinski, pretty in her finest regalia, positioned herself in front of her prisoner. She clutched onto a walking stick—a natural addition to her person after all those years clutching onto ski poles. While the dress was pleasant, Sister Agatha felt that the orange eyeliner was distracting but thought it might not be to her advantage telling her as much.

Benedykta gestured towards Kacper to leave, and as soon as they were alone, she pulled up a chair and sat in front of Sister Agatha.

'My friend tells me that you were eager to find me. He also says that he discovered a packet of rat poison hidden inside your pocket.'

Sister Agatha had hoped that that particular detail might go unnoticed. En route to Lazienki Park, she had passed a small hardware store and thought it would be an idea to invest in something that could be surreptitiously added to the proud grandmother's champagne flute during the celebrations. But, as Benedykta now held the small box aloft, she wagered that the rat poison would be her undoing instead.

'I was never too taken with math in school, Sister, but even I can put two and two together. From what I can tell, you were hoping to kill me today and destroy my poor great-granddaughter's special day.'

Benedykta pulled the lid off the box.

'My family is the most important thing in the world to me, Sister. I could never let anybody do anything to upset my beautiful Edyta,' she said, her intentions now extremely clear.

Rather abruptly, she jumped to her feet and violently ripped the tape off Sister Agatha's mouth before prising it open.

'That relation of yours – Olivier Guinot - who I killed eighty years ago deserved to die. How dare he attempt to take my darling, Herr Freudenberger, from me! And you can tell the bastard that when you see him in a few short minutes. You can also say hello to the three other people who, just like you, failed to succeed in ending the life of the great Benedykta Balinski!'

Sister Agatha wasn't sure if something was being lost in translation, but her instinct suggested that this megalomaniac had her confused with someone else. Weighing up the merits of explaining this to her, she ultimately decided that 'the great Benedykta Balinski' wasn't someone you might call a rational person.

'Please forgive me for having to do this so abruptly, but I have a bride-to-be waiting to be walked down the aisle.'

With that, she emptied the contents of the box into Sister Agatha's mouth, ensuring that the nun swallowed every last pellet. Job completed, Benedykta and her walking stick disappeared out the door, leaving her victim coughing and struggling to catch her breath. With only the mermaid in the square outside to keep her company in her final moments, this was not how Sister Agatha had expected her day to go. If she had eaten one of those apples after all, she might have had the strength to fight back.

FOURTEEN

Tymon Zinda grew up in Gdansk, a coastal city in northern Poland. Despite living in a pleasant spot, Tymon did not have a happy childhood, mainly because his horrid teacher left him petrified. The shy boy hoped that as soon as he turned ten and entered double digits, he would be able to stand up for himself once and for all, but, if anything, things only got worse. It seemed that Pan Malak became even more wicked the older the child became. Instead of one clip around the ear every time he missed an answer, Tymon now received two. Instead of getting two detentions for being late for school, Tymon would now get three. (Not that it was even his fault—his father had a van that 'broke down more often than a menopausal woman,' as Pan Malak would often joke).

With the school inspector set to visit one Thursday afternoon, the class was under strict instructions to be on its best behaviour, leaving twenty-four young pupils terrified that they would let Pan Malak down. Tymon Zinda did not sleep for an entire week leading up to the arrival of the special guest. On the big day, as the class smiled and recited their poetry in front of the surprisingly sweet inspector, Tymon felt a pressing need to go to the toilet. Being diabetic, the young fellow had this urge more often than most, but even though he was about to burst, he knew that that would be a better outcome than the punishment Pan Malak would dish out for interrupting the poetry presentation. Tymon crossed his legs and squeezed them together for dear life.

He probably would have made it to the end of class if the inspector hadn't asked Tymon to write the name of his favourite poet on the blackboard. As soon as Tymon stood up, the floodgates opened—the results of which were seen by all. After the inspector left, Pan Malak marched a mortified Tymon around every classroom and forced him to describe the dirty deed he had just done to his peers. Tymon was mocked, ridiculed, and taunted by the entire school from that day forth. With no friends, Tymon depended on his pet rat, Wiga, for companionship.

About a year following the unfortunate classroom incident, Tymon's father moved the family to Warsaw, where he opened a hardware store on Plac Defilad, one of the city's central squares. Delighted to start anew, Tymon and Wiga packed their belongings, jumped in the back of his father's new and improved van, and set off for the bright lights of Warsaw. Things at his next school proved more successful than in his last, but it can take a while for even the most confident newcomer to find their voice. Instead of playing football with the boys in his class after school, Tymon helped out in the hardware store, where he enjoyed the banter with the customers. That was until a tall and po-faced hotelier popped in looking for some rat poison. His building was overrun with the damned pests, and there was a pre-wedding drinks reception planned that evening for the city's most famous A-list couple, Edyta Balinski and Pawel Dragon, so he needed the property to be rodent-free!

Tymon couldn't believe his ears: why on earth would anyone want to kill a rat—what if they were a mother, father or sibling to his beloved Wiga? When this horrible monster had received what he needed and vanished out the door again, Tymon decided that moving forward, he would have to protect his furry best friend and all his kin. As his father enjoyed some pierogi one evening for dinner, Tymon crept downstairs into the store. Here, he emptied all the rat poison containers down the toilet and then filled them with rice that he had coloured green.

The next afternoon, Tymon, along with Wiga, sat in the store with one eye on his homework, the other on the door. When an elderly nun entered looking for some poison, Tymon held his breath, fearful that she and his father would notice that the containers had been tampered with. He closed his eyes shut and said a prayer that, for once, luck would be on his side. When the boy opened them again, the nun and her little packet of non-poisonous rice were gone, and no one was the wiser.

* * *

When Sister Agatha realised the poison that she had been sold in the hardware store that afternoon was nothing more sinister than uncooked rice dipped in some green colouring, she had a good mind to return there and demand her zloty back. Instead, she decided to cut her losses and get the hell out of Poland as quickly as she could—and while she could. Of course, she had no intention of letting Benedykta Balinski off scot-free (*how dare she attempt to poison me!*), but now that her cover was blown, she needed time—and space—to put together a more thorough plan. With Benedykta's cronies lurking at every corner, Warsaw was not a friend of Sister Agatha's at present—as charming as the city appeared to be. No, she needed to take care of herself before taking care of others, so to speak.

Now there was just the tiny matter of freeing herself from this uncomfortable chair and disappearing before Kacper or those rotten apple suppliers realised that their captive was still ripe for the picking. With the one remaining ounce of strength that she had left, Sister Agatha tugged and pulled at the rope. After rattling off a list of objects that she wished she had—a sharp knife, a firelighter, garden shears—she looked around the sparse space but couldn't find anything of use. She momentarily contemplated praying, but as gracious as the good Lord tended to be, she doubted that even He would be too forgiving of her antics over the past few days.

Looking at the window in front of her, she wondered whether she could hobble over, shatter the pane and, possibly, get the attention of some kind passer-by? Of course, she didn't want to be impolite to her hostess by vandalising the property but seeing as said woman had tried to murder her, etiquette was out the window—which is where she now hoped her elbow would go. The nun slowly but surely inched her way forward, resembling a disorientated and slow-moving grasshopper. It was far from an enjoyable exercise, but if Jesus, bruised and battered, could walk to Calvary with a cross on his back, she could successfully manage this short distance. The sweat and tears cascaded down her face, but Sister Agatha ploughed forward, one step at a time, and after what could only be described as an eternity, she was finally at arm's length from the window—only that her arms weren't available to her on this occasion. Her shoulders and right elbow were, and with one final heave, she lined the right side of her body against the pane and prepared herself to smash it.

'One, two, three, and—'

Following a couple of valiant but failed attempts, Sister Agatha thought it would be far more appropriate for the sheet of glass to be called a window pain, for that's what she felt trying to shatter it. Biting her lip, she persisted, but as her efforts continued to flounder, she stopped, eventually conceding defeat. Taking a moment to catch her breath, the nun racked her brain for an alternative method—if only she were in her prime, she would shuffle out the door, hop down the stairs and escape out the front entrance. But she wasn't—she was one-hundred-and-eighteen years old, with only a few days left to live. Her heavy head fell in front of her, and a multitude of thoughts raced through her mind—one, in particular: her vow to become the oldest person in the world remained unfulfilled.

Just as distressing was the realisation that the Order of Saint Aloysius would now need to fundraise from here until doomsday for that new kitchen, seeing as she had ransacked their kitty to fund her expedition.

And all for nothing.

She took a series of laboured breaths to energise herself but could feel her body slowing down, readying itself for the off. Darkness. Then suddenly, Sister Agatha's eyes flickered open, and she caught sight of her treasured emerald ring—an object that possessed more strength than a hundred hectares of spinach.

'Don't be such a naysayer!' she shouted. 'If all of these years on this earth has taught you anything, it's never to give up. Now, dust yourself off and get the hell out of here!'

She released a deep, guttural roar and, with the energy of a grizzly bear, doubled over. With the chair now on her back, knees bent, she shuffled towards the opened door—at a snail's pace, granted—and continued out onto the landing. The steep stairs looked tricky to negotiate, but with this new lease of life, Sister Agatha was now game for any challenge. Taking one step at a time, she edged closer and closer to freedom. A deluge of sweat continued to pour from her brow; the muscles in her legs and thighs were ablaze.

Finally, this unyielding Irish warrior landed in the damp and dark hallway below. Mere metres before reaching the front door, she heard a car pulling into the backyard. She had previously suspected that Kacper had chauffeured Benedykta back to Lazienki Park in time to accompany the bride-to-be down the aisle and now imagined that the backstabbing, double-dealing air steward was returning to dispose of her body.

No time to hang around, so!

With fists of fury, Sister Agatha made one final push forward, down the hallway and towards the exit—almost putting her head through the wall in the process. Having reached the door, she lowered her mouth towards the lock and attempted to pry it open, but it wasn't obliging. She could see that rust had set in from infrequent usage—a point that was proving most inconvenient, seeing as she had only seconds left to succeed in her breakout.

Fearful that the key would be her Waterloo, she abandoned any designs of convincing it to do its one job. Sister Agatha hobbled a few paces backwards and stopped. There was no time for deep breathing or motivational talks—she had just seconds to liberate herself before Kacper entered the hallway.

'One, two—'

And without waiting for 'three', Sister Agatha shut her eyes, charged across the hallway, and smashed through the rickety, rotting door before thrusting herself out into the daylight. Free at long last! (But how her body ached!)

With the help of her new pal, adrenaline, she hurried over to her old pal, the Mermaid of Warsaw. After placing her chair onto the ground beside the statue, she dropped her head to the side and took a brief but much-deserved breather. When Sister Agatha eventually blinked open her eyes again, she looked around, expecting to see a crowd lining up to free her from the chair. While a cluster of curious tourists had indeed formed around her, they were under the impression that the nun was a street performer about to entertain them with a quirky routine—and not the victim of a brutal kidnapping.

Moments later, looks of disappointment crossed their faces when they realised that the headline act had fallen fast asleep, understandably exhausted from her great escape.

* * *

THE WARSAW POST, 14 MARCH 2016

Poland will hold a state funeral for the country's oldest citizen, Benedykta Balinski, who finally succumbed to death on Sunday at the glorious age of 121. She will be laid to rest in the Alley of Honour at the Powazki military cemetery in Warsaw on 18 March.

Balinski was attending her great-granddaughter's wedding to multi-millionaire Pawel Dragon and surrendered to a massive heart attack following the evening reception. As the Polish legend was making her way to her car at the end of the night, witnesses reported that three French dancers insisted that she return to the marquee and join them in their can-can routine. Never one to say no, the much-loved figure agreed, removed her high heels before jumping onto the stage with them.

At first, Balinski proved a natural, completely capable of keeping up with the three exotic professionals. As the music suddenly sped up, it became apparent that the former Olympic medalist was struggling for breath. Even more tragic, it appeared that the three dancers were dedicating the lively routine to their own late great-grandparent. At one stage, they turned to the crowd and shouted:

'*Ceci est pour la mort de notre arrière-grand-père, Oliver Guinot!*' ('This is for our great-grandfather's death, Oliver Guinot!')

Rather poignantly, *The Warsaw Post* can now confirm that this deceased relative was, like Balinski, a war hero who was murdered near the Seine in Paris by a German Nazi during the Second World War.

Balinski was widely respected in her beloved Poland, both as an athlete and a war veteran. Working as a spy, the fearless patriot was known to have played a vital role in the Allies' victory over Nazi Germany.

Following Balinski's death, the Polish president tweeted that the news had deeply saddened him. He wrote: 'It's a tremendous loss, a great Pole has departed our great country :-('

FIFTEEN

* * *

Venice would have been Sister Agatha's immediate reply if someone were to ask her where she would most like to visit in the world. Based on her reading over the decades, she thought the one-time maritime dynasty, with its meandering canals, delicate bridges and bobbing gondolas, sounded only otherworldly. Sipping on an expensive Cappuccino outside Caffè Florian and watching tourists vie for space in the crowded Piazza San Marco—a square that a certain diminutive French emperor once christened the 'drawing

124

room of Europe'— she knew her instincts about the city were well-founded.

The much-admired Caffè Florian didn't just refresh weary souls; it also entertained them, thanks to their lively house band that helped in a small way to justify the establishment's exorbitant prices. Despite the cost, the elderly patron wasted no time ordering a second coffee—she was desperate to cling to this captivating experience for another few moments but, more importantly, was in dire need of a caffeine fix. Having fallen asleep in Warsaw's Old Town, Sister Agatha hadn't awoken until six o'clock the following morning—and that was only because some pesky street cleaners were unaccommodating. In fact, her slumber had been so intense that she missed the earlier drama on the square: Kasper, who had been chasing his prisoner following her brave escape, didn't notice an oncoming delivery truck and was knocked down—just like the dummy he had previously hit outside the airport. While doctors predicted he would rally, the same couldn't be said for one of the city's other residents.

It was en route to the airport—whilst attempting to iron out the creak in her neck and remove the ants from inside her veil— that Sister Agatha discovered the fate of Benedykta Balinski. (She knew those French dancers that she first met in Charles de Gaulle airport a few days earlier would be allies!) The news had equipped her with enough energy to reach her final destination: Venice, the Queen of the Adriatic Sea.

Sister Agatha had soon found herself exhausted once again. After alighting the airport vaporetto at San Zaccaria, it had taken her close to two hours to walk the short distance to where she now sat in Saint Mark's Square. The majesty of the Doge's Palace, along with the loftiness of the Bridge of Sighs, the grandeur of Saint Mark's Basilica and the monumental authority of the Campanile, left her overwhelmed—and in desperate need of as much coffee as she could get her hands on. (And yes, she remained on a budget, but given the news concerning Benedytka's demise, she felt a little treat or two was in order.)

Earlier, as she passed the aforementioned Doge's Palace, she had noticed that two of the pillars on the balcony were not the same off-white colour as their neighbouring counterparts but, instead, a faded red.

'The blood-like colour you see there marked the spot where convicts were publicly hanged in the years gone by,' a tour guide had announced to a suitably horrified group of American tourists. 'Apparently, it was a common undertaking that also served to remind the city's residents that there were repercussions for all transgressions!'

Today, Sister Agatha hoped that she could continue this spirited murdering tradition. When in Venice, after all!

As she waited for the barista to work his magic, the nun observed the onslaught of pigeons roaming the square, demanding to be fed by passers-by. But the winged rodents, as Sister Consuela would refer to them, didn't bother Sister Agatha in the slightest, even as they loitered around her feet or perched themselves on her little table. Not even an earthquake would have been able to interfere with the pleasure she received from the surrounding architectural treasures.

As the waiter arrived with her second coffee and second amaretto biscuit, Sister Agatha couldn't help but release a giddy laugh. She was now just a hair's breadth away from being the oldest person in the world and, almost equally as thrilling, she was in Venice, drinking Cappuccinos! While she loved Navan's Ardboyne Hotel, where she would usually enjoy this particular beverage each month after her visit to Doctor McManus, the nun knew that her current coffee-drinking experience could never be topped. She dropped the amber biscuit into the Cappuccino and watched it slowly dissolve.

Let's hope Riccardo will disappear just as easily, she joked, taking a large, inelegant slurp. If not...

The past number of days had the makings of a three-act opera, but Sister Agatha had a feeling that the best was yet to come. And while she was soon to go the way of all flesh, like Pompeii some seven-hundred-and-forty kilometres due south, she was determined to go out with a bang.

126

* * *

Sister Agatha knew that there was work to be done but couldn't resist taking a brief stroll around Venice's web of narrow, cobbled vie. In terms of exercise, she was undoubtedly receiving value for money, crossing an endless number of bridges that linked these streets. The city's surreal, film-like atmosphere gave way to imaginings of being a wealthy noblewoman living in one of the luxurious palazzi dotting the city. What a sight she would be, kitted out in an outlandish dress replete with luscious velvet and precious silk—with an ornate mask to complete the look. How the sisters in the convent would have laughed! (Sister Concepta, on the other hand, might have cried. Such a scene would indeed have brought back painful memories of the time when the Venetian-styled dresses she'd spent a year making for a school production of *Othello* had been thrown in a skip by the overzealous caretaker.)

Just as she indulged in this frivolous fantasy, Sister Agatha passed a costumier's shop, its windows filled with the regalia she was daydreaming about. Battling temptation, she hovered in front of the doorway. Did she dare discard the armour that had served her so well for nearly a hundred years in favour of something more fabulous, say?

It's time to break a 'habit' of a lifetime, she joked, crossing the threshold into a store that would have left Marie Antoinette in a swoon. (Besides, the nun had noticed something malodorous since her arrival in the city, and she wasn't sure if it were the fetid canals or her clothes.)

As Sister Agatha waded through the sea of fabrics and caught sight of the price tags, the high spirits that she had initially felt soon evaporated, and in its place came a familiar heavy and guilty heart. While she couldn't have become the second-oldest person in the world—and in a few hours, God willing, the oldest—without a budget, her biggest regret since fleeing Navan five days earlier was pillaging the convent's bank account. She had seen first-hand how much effort they had put into raising funds for Sister Josephine's kitchen. Just because it was a necessary evil didn't mean that she had to be proud of her actions.

Before she expired, Sister Agatha decided there and then to pay back every cent—somehow. But until that moment arrived, she was determined to return to the thriftiness that had previously stood in her good stead. No more eighteen-euro coffees—and certainly no expensive dresses like those surrounding her. Steadfast in her decision, she turned on her heels and marched towards the exit but was stopped by a shop assistant, holding aloft a floor-length, taffeta ball gown, complete with an embroidered corset.

'*Lo provi pure,*' the assistant insisted, stroking the layers upon layers of delicate lace ruffles.

Well, there's no harm trying it on, is there?

No, there most certainly wasn't, Sister Agatha convinced herself before disappearing behind the curtain to investigate if she would have made for a convincing *gentildonna* after all.

* * *

Vivienne Taylor took her first breath in Darwin, Australia, on Christmas Eve 1974, the same day Cyclone Tracy had kicked up a storm in the city. In tribute to this environment, Vivienne spent the following forty-odd years causing irreparable damage to the lives of almost everyone she crossed. For instance, at twelve years of age, Vivienne played in a pool in her back garden when she noticed her neighbour happily tending to his lilies. Wanting money for an upcoming school tour, she waltzed over to him, devil may care, and ripped off part of her bikini.

'If you don't give me five dollars, I will tell my parents that you did this to me.'

The neighbour was stunned, and even though he was not remotely interested in pre-pubescent girls, he didn't want to take his chances with Vivienne's father, who was known throughout the town for his violent behaviour. He fished out his wallet and gave his accuser the money she had demanded. Delighted at the ease with which she had increased her funds, Vivienne felt confident that she had now found her calling in life. Over the following years, her piggy bank prospered while the reputations of innocent men did not.

When Vivienne reached her thirties, the determined

entrepreneur thought it was high time she upskilled and expanded her business. She found employment as a maître d' on a luxurious yacht that travelled in and out of Venice. Long gone were the days when she was bartering over five dollars; now, discussions revolved around sums that involved at least four digits. (If such numbers weren't readily available, Vivienne made do with their wives' diamonds and pearls instead.)

This deception continued for many years, but complacency and arrogance soon set in, and Vivienne started getting too big for her designer boots. After secretly filming an intimate exchange between herself and a wealthy Polish entrepreneur called Pawel Dragon, Vivienne demanded two hundred thousand euro to keep mum. Seeing as he was just months away from marrying into a family whose head had bravely fought on behalf of Poland during the Second World War, there was no way that Pawel would bow down and acquiesce willy-nilly.

That night, as the music of local-boy Vivaldi seduced the future Mrs Dragon in one of Venice's many churches, Pawel arranged to meet his blackmailer at the Venetian Arsenal—a cluster of shipyards and armouries that offered an abundance of privacy. Armed with a pistol, as she always was, Vivienne waited by the Porta Magna—the brightly lit entrance—and tried to silence the roars of her gut, which were telling her that something was amiss. When twenty minutes passed, and Pawel still hadn't shown up, that initial anxiety turned to fury.

How dare he be so arrogant as to make a fool of me?

Vivienne was about to return to the cruise ship where she planned to spill some scandalous beans when she heard a whistle from someone onboard a tiny boat in a nearby canal.

'I have your money,' the voice cried out.

It was Pawel. Vivienne marched over in his direction to give him what for when she felt a blow to the head, then nothing.

When Vivienne eventually regained consciousness, her mouth was taped while her two hands were handcuffed to the rail of a boat, in which she sat alone. It bobbed up and down on the lagoon, away from its main thoroughfare but, she hoped, still within some rescuer's range of vision. After a few moments, Vivienne noticed a second boat speeding in her direction: was it friend or foe? The answer soon became apparent when it pulled up beside her—in it sat Pawel, holding Vivienne's very own pistol. He jumped onto her boat, and even though his presence meant only one thing, Vivienne was surprised by how calm she felt—almost as if she had expected this day to come. Even when he dangled the pistol in front of her face, she barely flinched. But Pawel didn't shoot her; instead, he shot a hole in the boat's floor.

'It was nice doing business with you,' he said, almost spitting the words in her face before disappearing to learn his fiancée's thoughts on *The Four Seasons*.

As her boat slowly vanished under the lagoon, Vivienne's final thoughts focused not on her downfall but on the windfall she had accumulated over the decades and what might come of her secret stash. For somebody in Vivienne's occupation, opening a mainstream savings account in which she could squirrel away her ill-gotten gains was not an option. So, ever the pragmatist, she hid her money in the lining of a big, flouncy period dress that she had found in a wardrobe in her rented apartment. At the time, she took comfort in the fact that the elaborate outfit comprised of so many layers of material that not even the city's venerated Marco Polo would have either the expertise or patience to discover what she had hidden within it.

As the boat sank lower and lower, she now feared that she might have been

too smart for her own good. Vivienne estimated that she had accumulated well over a million euro due to a lifetime being engaged in questionable deeds—more than enough for her benefactor to transform their life. But how would they find it? Maybe her old landlord would flog the dress to some local costumier who would, in turn, sell it to some charitable soul who would, in turn, put the money stashed in it to good use by helping those in need—a kind nun, perhaps?

Aware that she was in no position to make plea bargains with the man above, Vivienne nonetheless stormed heaven and quickly rattled off a short prayer—her first since childhood. She begged whoever might be listening to allow the million euro to find its way into the right hands. That her life of crime might soon benefit others gave Vivienne great comfort as she took her last breath before vanishing under the lagoon's murky waters.

SIXTEEN

Following a quick trip to a bank where Sister Agatha made a million-euro deposit into the convent's account—thanks to the now unstoppable generosity of Lady Luck (and, she imagined, the forgetfulness of the money's previous owner)—the debt-free and conscience-free nun boarded her second vaporetto of the day. Decked out in her splendid new outfit, she had happily played the role of fawning tourist for the past number of hours (the majestic Rialto Bridge overlooking the Grand Canal was especially pleasant to visit). Now, it was time to return to the business at hand.

Her destination was Lido, an affluent island located a short ferry ride from Venice. Scattered across the city's lagoon were one-hundred-and-eighteen islands ('my exact age!' Sister Agatha shouted to passers-by when she read the statistic on a leaflet), and Lido was, by far, the largest. Even with her limited Italian, Sister Agatha knew that the island's name translated as 'beach' and wondered if she would get an opportunity to dip her feet into the Adriatic Sea. The salt would work wonders on her many blisters and bunions.

Convinced that her new, showy apparel would turn the heads of fellow passengers, she was soon left disappointed when the only attention it received was from one over-friendly dog. The little poodle became so comfortable amongst the layers that Sister Agatha suspected he was on the verge of marking his newfound territory. She had little interest in rocking up to her fourth and final victim smelling like poor Sister Mildred after the Alzheimer's had kicked in, so she quickly swatted the curious canine away.

For locals, such ferry journeys were simply a means of getting from A to B. For Sister Agatha and, she suspected, every other visitor of the Floating City, it was akin to a five-star cruise—without those exorbitant prices to boot! Over the twenty-minute duration, she stood facing Venice and allowed the sun to shine on her skin, although, thanks to her tinted glasses, she could admire the splendid Saint George's Island and the golden bronze wind vane that crowned the city's customs house, Dogana di Mare.

Suppose this particular visitor was to make a complaint, it would be the abrupt manner the ferry pulled into the various stops. It was almost a case of 'Nun overboard!' on more than one occasion. When the ferry finally reached *terra firma*, it took the visitor just a few footsteps to learn that Lido possessed many fine assets, notably a portfolio of lavish villas. It was also home to one of the most talked-about celebrations of celluloid in the world: the Venice Film Festival. But Sister Agatha wasn't on the lookout for Hollywood's finest; her only interest was in another star—the oldest person in the world. She wanted to take his life and then take his title. After emerging from the ferry terminal onto the island, Sister Agatha quickly hailed a taxi and set off to finish the job she had started five days earlier in Tunisia.

* * *

Even though Riccardo Trentini had walked the earth longer than anyone else alive (although, in more recent times, 'slowly hobbled' would have been a more accurate description), precious little was known about the world's oldest man - particularly his early years. In the many articles that documented his remarkable existence, there appeared to be a consensus that the one-hundred-and-twenty-one-year-old's story had started when he arrived in Florence, the art capital of the world.

Here, in the city that Michelangelo's *David* called home, a twenty-year-old Riccardo worked as an apprentice sculptor in the studio of a respected master for a handful of years, learning his trade and honing his craft. He then went to Venice with his mentor, who had received a year-long commission from a wealthy politician to create a sculpture of his family. A single day was all Riccardo needed to know that Venice was where he wanted to spend his life.

There had been no wives, children or fortune—just love for his work, which had proven to be highly successful in his newly adopted home. The commissions quickly arrived, although many observers felt Riccardo was missing a good manager or art dealer, seeing as the sculptor himself had been grossly undercharging for his work. But Venice's adopted son had never wanted for much in life—so long as he had enough money for a drop of Limoncello at the end of a long day at the studio, he was more than happy. After all, the sculptor had been gifted the most magnificent talent—what else could he possibly want?

When he marched into his eighty-fifth year, Riccardo's body suddenly decided that it had had its fill of life on top of a ladder, chiselling marble and clay. On the instructions of his doctor, he moved to Stella della Laguna, a well-respected residential home for the elderly on the nearby island of Lido, a place where he was expected to stay temporarily. While the doctor initially informed the owners that the prognosis for Riccardo wasn't encouraging, the stubborn artist had been there ever since—some thirty-six years later.

Of course, there's no such thing as a free lunch, so after reams of red tape conveniently disappeared out of harm's way, the owner of Stella della Laguna had been granted permission to sell Riccardo's wares. (After the sculptor had passed the hundred mark, there was quite the uptick in the value of his stock). While Riccardo had accumulated an impressive body of work over the years, his persistence in living meant that Stella della Laguna had little left to flog off in recent years.

Naturally, they didn't want their most famed resident to die over something as vulgar as money—but nor did they want him to outstay his welcome either.

* * *

After a short taxi journey had turned into a long taxi journey thanks to the many pitstops Sister Agatha made to photograph the splendid lagoon and wisteria-covered villas, Lido's latest arrival finally sauntered into Stella della Laguna. As she entered the domed-roof reception area, Sister Agatha was initially tickled by how perfectly her costume mirrored the effortlessly chic, periwinkle-blue interiors. On the verge of reclining on a red velvet chaise longue hidden in an alcove, Sister Agatha suddenly remembered she wasn't here to act like Lady Muck. No, she was here on essential business, and because she had been too busy sightseeing or admiring the local ladies' designer garb, Sister Agatha hadn't yet decided on how best to carry out the murder.

(She had also treated her driver to some delicious *tramezzini* sandwiches that were winking at her from a glass display in one of the island's many bars. So heavenly were the prawn and crab options that the hungry nun had four in total!)

In her defence, the hijinks over the past five days would have taken their toll on even the hardiest of souls, so it was no wonder that she was not firing on all cylinders. Even still, there was no excuse for sloppiness, particularly as she'd escaped Warsaw by the skin of her false teeth. Determined not to falter at the final hurdle, Sister Agatha now decided to return to Stella della Laguna when she had adequately hatched a plan. Moments earlier, she had spotted a bench hidden underneath a maritime pine tree, overlooking a cluster of small islands; the nun decided to take refuge there until she found inspiration for her dirty deed.

Before she could make this discreet U-turn, a grey-haired receptionist emerged from a small office and, arms outstretched, gave Sister Agatha a royal welcome.

'*Benvenuta!*' she exclaimed. '*È qui per vedere qualcuno di importante?*'

Sister Agatha's knowledge of Italian was limited, so she hadn't the foggiest idea of what was being said to her.

'I'm here to visit an old friend,' Sister Agatha improvised. 'His name is Riccardo Trentini.'

As soon as she uttered those two words, a most peculiar thing happened. The receptionist's breathing became manic; her cheeks flushed. She quickly hurried across the foyer and took Sister Agatha by the arm, dragging her down the corridor.

'*Madonna!* We knew you would come,' the receptionist gushed, fighting back the tears. 'Ludovico knew you would come! We all did!'

While Sister Agatha had always enjoyed the convent's annual sports day, being dragged through Stella della Laguna in a hybrid between tug-a-war and a wheelbarrow race proved most unpleasant for the super-centenarian.

'Promise me you won't be disappointed if he doesn't recognise you, though,' the unhinged receptionist added in between breaths, her voice afire. 'You probably aren't even aware of how old he is at this stage.'

Funny you should mention that…

They finally arrived at an open door and stopped. Sister Agatha leaned against the wall to catch her breath, but the receptionist had little interest in breaks. After giving Sister Agatha one final smile, she took her by the arm again and led her into the bedroom.

'*Riccardo, c'è qualcuno per Lei,*' the receptionist informed him, although this news that somebody had come to visit him received no acknowledgement.

Instead, the world's oldest person faced the window, looking out onto the calm Adriatic Sea. The receptionist gestured to Sister Agatha to take a seat beside him. '*Per favore*—I know you have dressed up so beautifully for your reunion—and how lovely your curls are—but don't expect too much from him; it has been a long time since he last spoke. Like I say, it is unlikely that he will recognise you.'

As a baffled Sister Agatha moved towards him, the receptionist returned to the door, and when a cleaner passed in the corridor, she barked at him to fetch someone called Ludovico.

'*Pronto! Pronto!*'

Sister Agatha wondered if it were the day off for the staff at Stella della Laguna with the residents being given the run of the place because this lady appeared to have a colony of bats in the belfry. Who did she think Sister Agatha was? When the visitor returned her attention to Riccardo—the only person preventing her from fulfilling her vow—the pandemonium faded away. Instead, she felt a quiet melancholy overtake her. When society conjured up images of people over a hundred years old, they pictured the barely functioning variety, folk who should be revered and respected but who, ultimately, should be treated like a dusty ornament in someone's glass menagerie. While Sister Agatha always felt she had successfully challenged this profile, looking at Riccardo Trentini slumped in front of her, she soon realised that stereotypes often existed for a reason.

What's more, she now thought it would be regrettable if even one droplet of blood had to be spilt during the disposal of her unsuspecting rival—after all, Riccardo looked lovely and serene and undeserving of anything so vulgar. Maybe he would be a rational and an obliging gentleman who could be convinced to shed his mortal coil sooner rather than later? After all, it wasn't as if a world of adventure awaited the poor creature in his current state.

Just as she was about to plead her case, Sister Agatha was struck by the surrounding art and felt like she could have been sitting in a museum. Whoever his muse was, Riccardo undoubtedly harboured an obsession because he had celebrated her in each of these four sculptures. But she wasn't there to admire art, the nun reminded herself, and moved the chair directly in front of her prey - the only person in the entire world who was preventing her from achieving her goal. Sister Agatha surveyed his sunken, hollow face, but his eyes didn't flinch; Riccardo was only inches away from her, but he may as well have been thousands of miles.

'*Ciao*,' she said softly.

'You might not think it,' the receptionist interjected, a note of pride in her voice, 'his heart is that of a man fifty years younger than him. *I m*edici say he could live another few years if he remains this peaceful.'

On hearing this prognosis, Sister Agatha didn't even attempt to hide her disappointment.

'I hope you know how important you were to him,' the receptionist continued, misinterpreting Sister Agatha's heavy heart and pointing towards a small sculpture that stood by his bed. 'He kept you close to him all this time. Unfortunately, a few years ago, the director of Stella della Laguna auctioned most of his work, but Ludovico insisted that those few remain here.'

The receptionist then lowered her head, ashamed of what she was about to utter.

'Sadly, these pieces are now due to be auctioned off sometime next week. The director... He has to....' She could barely bring herself to say it. 'Money. For Riccardo's sake, I hope he doesn't know what's happening—it would break his heart. And yours, too, no?'

Sister Agatha wasn't quite grasping what this crazy receptionist was chattering on about, but she was tiring of her nonsense. Couldn't she go away and make herself useful by helping one of the residents with their daily crosswords or cleaning the mildew out of the cobwebs?

'I always imagined it must have been difficult being a model for an artist—having to remain frozen for so long,' the receptionist continued, trying to leaven the mood. 'I can barely keep still for un secondo!'

Sister Agatha was about to give this irritating woman short shrift when it suddenly dawned on her what was being said. Initially, it seemed so ludicrous that she wondered if her new corset was pulled too tightly, starving her brain of much-needed oxygen. But as she scanned the room, there appeared to be truth in what was being suggested. The nun slowly walked towards one of the examples of Riccardo's extraordinary artwork that rested on his bedside locker. She removed her tinted glasses to make sure that what she thought she was seeing was true.

When she had overheard her diagnosis in Navan several days ago, a multitude of thoughts ran through her mind, notably what was in store for her in her final days. But she most definitely didn't expect to be standing in a nursing home on an island just off the coast of Venice—staring back at herself.

'We have been wondering for years who she was,' the receptionist revealed, drawing closer to her. 'And now you have arrived. *Non ci credo.*'

Sister Agatha couldn't believe what she was hearing—or seeing—either.

'*Aspetti qui!* We all want to hear the real story, especially

Ludovico. He will be here in *un mo*mento. You must tell us how you fell in love. Will you? Ludovico is going to burst with happiness! Just wait *un momento!*'

The receptionist vanished, leaving Sister Agatha alone—she tightly held the emerald ring that hung from her rosary beads. Even though she hadn't prepared herself for this visit, the last thing she anticipated doing was telling Stella della Laguna's staff and residents—and this Ludovico chap—about her childhood and one true love, Pádraig Keogh.

* * *

Ludovico Bianchi was a hopeless romantic. There was nothing that excited him more than a good love story. Since childhood, each September during the Venice Film Festival, he would stand outside the stylish Cinema Palace for hours on end. Here, he watched stars like Juliette Binoche or River Phoenix pose for the cameras in their splendid gowns and dapper tuxedos.

When he wasn't outside the cinema, he was loitering around the nearby Moorish Excelsior Hotel, which housed these VIPs, and when he glimpsed them, Ludovico would wave as if they were his long-lost friends. Having watched almost every romantic comedy ever made, he would always project himself onto the shoulders of their stars, convinced that he was one of the characters onscreen. He would laugh with them, cry with them and cheer them on, unable to distinguish between fact and fiction.

In real life, things weren't quite so peachy. Possessing good looks, Ludovico attracted many male admirers. To begin with, these men were quite bemused by his romantic inclinations. But when it transpired that Ludovico's understanding of intimacy was limited to a kiss and cuddle (why sully matters by getting unpleasant bodily fluids involved?), those red-blooded men called 'cut' on their relationship with the film buff.

'No worries!' was Ludovico's response, deciding that the Johnny Depps and George Clooneys of the world were more than enough for his beating heart. His mother had often demanded to know when to expect grandchildren; Signora Bianchi died waiting.

The very minute Ludovico joined the staff of Stella della Laguna as an eighteen-year-old, he became infatuated with the mysterious Riccardo Trentini. When the nurse wasn't busy with the duties he was employed to do, he would spend his hours daydreaming about the beautiful muse in his work. Her delicate features were so precise and life-like that Ludovico was convinced she had to be more than just some model the sculptor randomly found on the streets; she must have been his love—his soul mate.

Every day, Ludovico would conjure up different possibilities for what happened between the pair. Maybe the young lady had been in an unhappy marriage to some influential politician or statesman, and their love was forbidden and clandestine? Could it be that they were two teenage lovebirds and after she had become pregnant with his child, her deeply religious parents sent her away to a rich aunt in the mountains, never to be seen again? Or perhaps she had been struck down with tuberculosis, and they hastily married moments before she had died in his arms. Oh, the tragedy!

But the theory the nurse indulged most was his interpretation of why Riccardo stared so intently out the window, day in, day out. Ludovico decided that he was waiting for the love of his life to return, and the reason they had been kept apart was down to a simple misunderstanding. They had planned to run away, but someone—like a jealous, overbearing parent—had done something wretched to prevent them from disappearing into the night together. Ludovico knew that the gifted artist had not given up hope and, as such, neither would he.

Every day for over two decades, when the thirty-eight-year-old arrived at work, he would inquire if Riccardo had welcomed any visitors. Even though he never received a favourable response, he always needed a minute to regroup after being told that the sculptor remained alone. But once there's life, there's hope, and there was a reason this brilliant man was refusing to die: he was living for someone; he was living for love.

Ludovico sat in the kitchen with a few of his colleagues, eating the leftover birthday cake made for one of the residents, when the cleaner, followed by the receptionist, came rushing in with the news.

'*È arrivata! È arrivata!*'

Ludovico spat out the masticated sponge, making a sorry mess of the lovely canteen table in the process. He couldn't believe his ears: could it be true? Had Riccardo's one true love finally arrived?

'*È arrivata! È arrivata!*' the receptionist repeated.

Ludovico had always known that God was good; he knew that He wouldn't fail him. He knew that his endless prayers, rosaries and novenas would be answered one day—and now it seemed as if that 'one day' had arrived.

Unable to handle the excitement, Ludovico went into a state of shock and remained rooted to the chair, staring directly in front of him. His bewildered colleagues looked at each other, wondering if they should call for one of the doctors. The nurse's hands suddenly started to shake; his legs trembled. Sometimes, the only reason he got out of bed in the morning was in the belief that this particular moment would come to fruition. Now that it was here, he didn't know how to act.

Without knowing what else to do, the nurse furiously wolfed down every last morsel of the cake—his face covered in chocolate, cream and multi-coloured sprinkles. Now fuelled and ready to go, the man slowly rose to his feet and took a deep breath. Then, with a speed that would put a blush on the cheeks of a cheetah, he sprinted out of the canteen and down the hall to meet the lady who had captured Riccardo Trentini's heart many moons ago.

Better again, he was finally going to hear the real reason why they had been kept apart for so many years.

SEVENTEEN

Pádraig Keogh placed a large blanket under his bedsheets to give the impression that he was asleep. He didn't expect anyone would be checking in on him at this early hour, but the young swain wasn't taking any chances. He left a note for his mother under his pillow, one that explained his love for Butsy Miller—how it was real and vital and irrepressible, and that, without the teenager by his side, life wasn't worth a jot to him.

Content that everything was in order, Pádraig opened the window and disappeared across the field, his feet barely touching the ground beneath him. Approaching the village, he spotted a lone figure standing beneath the tree and was delighted that Butsy, too, was early. The sooner they could get out of Kilberry, the better. However, the closer he got, the less convinced he became that it was his fiancée who was waiting; the figure appeared to be almost a foot taller and a couple of stone heavier. He slowed his pace until reaching a complete stop—his heart sank. Standing under the sycamore tree was not the most beautiful girl in the village; it was none other than his blasted mother.

After making a mental note to give big-mouthed Liam a good hiding when he next saw him, Pádraig attempted to compose himself. Even though he knew his mother would never entertain the union, the nineteen-year-old was determined that she wouldn't walk all over him anymore—something that she had been doing since he was born.

'You might stop me today, Mother; you might stop me tomorrow, but I am going to be with Butsy Miller one way or—'

'I'm dying,' Mrs Keogh interrupted—her voice for the first

time lacking the authority that everyone in the village had become so accustomed to hearing.

'What?'

'In a week, maybe a month, I will be gone,' she continued, her face unable to hide her fear. 'Then you'll be able to do whatever you please, with whoever you please.'

Pádraig didn't know what to think—or even how to feel; it seemed the pair did nothing other than cross swords, but that didn't mean he wanted her to die.

'The girls and I are going to your aunt's in County Wexford— the doctor thinks the sea air will help. I would love you, my only son, to be with me.'

Pádraig felt a knot zigzag in his stomach; he was being asked to choose.

'Of course, it's completely up to you,' she added.

A coughing fit suddenly overwhelmed her, and Mrs Keogh was forced to lean on the tree for support. He dashed over and rubbed her back to quench the fire that appeared to rage within her chest.

'Of course I'll come; of course I will,' he reassured her.

His mother looked up at him—her hardened face filled with unusual tenderness.

'After I'm gone, which probably will be quite soon, you can come back for Butsy. And, if you make her half as happy as you've made me over the years, she'll be a lucky woman.'

At once, Pádraig was heartbroken at the state of his mother's health but also giddy at the thought of Butsy being his wife. And rather than living hand to mouth in some godforsaken hovel, they would be able to create a family in the village they had loved so much.

'I must wait just half an hour to tell her—Butsy will understand. You go home, and I will join you shortly, and then we will make tracks to Aunty Jean's,' he instructed.

With the precision of a theatrical show, a troop of horses sounded, and a set of lanterns emerged from a carriage.

'We have to go now, Pádraig. Time isn't on my side—I'm not even sure if I'll have the strength to make it all the way to Wexford.'

And to corroborate her argument, another coughing fit presented itself, forcing her onto the ground, on all fours. Pádraig helped her into the carriage.

I'll write to Butsy, he decided. *As soon as we arrive, I'll tell her that I'll return to Kilberry in no time.*

Except he didn't return to Kilberry in no time at all because, funnily enough, his sick mother didn't surrender to her terminal illness as promised because there was, of course, no illness. Mrs Keogh would have stood in front of any jury in any courthouse and argued that, sometimes, mothers must act in extreme ways to protect their offspring, something she was doing by keeping him away from that 'peasant'.

To add insult to injury, Butsy never received the letter from Pádraig explaining why he had failed to show up as arranged—not to mention the other letters he had written to her daily over the following months. Mrs Keogh had given the postman a couple of bob to ensure they never reached her 'poor and dirty hands.'

When the Keoghs returned to Kilberry four months later, Butsy had joined the convent, much to Pádraig's dismay. After a night of drinking brandy, his mother revealed her duplicity. On hearing the revelations, he was just short of doing what Crazy Curly Weldon had done to his dog the week before: tying a rope around her neck and throwing her off a bridge. (But unlike Crazy Curly Weldon, Pádraig would ensure that he tied the knot properly and succeed in the terrible act.) But he ultimately decided that such an end would be too good for the evil beast and instead promised never to set foot in County Meath ever again. And sure enough, he remained true to his word.

Rather poetically, Mrs Keogh was killed the following Christmas after becoming captured in one of the many booby-traps that Crazy Curly Weldon randomly placed around the community. A herd of cows, who were being taken in from the cold by one of Mrs Keogh's seven unappealing—and still unmarried—daughters, trampled over her body, hidden in the tall grass. There was singing and dancing and merriment that night—not only in the local pub but also in the Keogh residence. Several years passed before the natural heir to the property heard about the bovine butchering because Pádraig had upped sticks and disappeared to Europe.

* * *

As Riccardo slept soundly on his bed, Sister Agatha, perched beside him, held the sparkling emerald ring aloft and finished her story. Her enraptured audience, packed into the room, wiped away the many tears that flooded their faces—poor Ludovico was nearly submerged in his. (What he would have done to that wretched Mrs Keogh if those heroic heifers hadn't gotten there first!)

'So, you never really wanted to be a nun?' one of the younger chefs, captivated by the tragic tale, demanded to know before being berated by an older colleague for questioning Sister Agatha's commitment to God. One of the residents then interjected; his husky voice suggested that he also enjoyed the odd cigarette or two like the late Sister Eithne.

'How did you hear about Pádraig's story?' one of the nurses asked, translating on his behalf. 'Did his letters make it to you in the end?'

Sister Agatha shook her head. 'No, I never received any of his correspondences—if I had, God only knows how different our stories might have turned out. I only heard what Mrs Keogh had done many years later—and by chance, if you can believe it.'

Ludovico, who had initially been so overwhelmed by Sister Agatha's arrival, not to mention the revelations that followed, eventually found his voice again and had little interest in keeping his emotions in check.

'I was *certo* that you would come for Riccardo—or should I now say "Pádraig"!' he gushed. 'I know he was sure that you would, too. Every day, without fail, he kept a faithful watch at that window, as if he was just waiting for the hour that you would be reunited! It's the most beautiful....'

He trailed off as the tears and emotions took over once again. After being comforted by those around him, he staggered to his feet. Like a newborn fawn, he slowly made his way over to their guest of honour before embracing her so tightly that one of the other staff members had to coax the nurse away.

'Eureka!' Ludovico screamed, nearly deafening everyone, including those at the front who were dependent on ineffective hearing aids. An extraordinary plan had just formed in his mind. It was the perfect finale to the remarkable tale of the two star-crossed lovers. 'Don't move a muscle, *Sorella*! I have an idea!'

* * *

On the day of Sister Agatha's visit, Paolo Scarpa, the director of Stella della Laguna, would not have looked out of place in an ashtray. Both his wiry hair and scaly skin were all shades of grey; his lips had long since disappeared into the crevices of his stubbly chin; his bloodshot eyes battled to remain open. Overseeing a struggling nursing home did not encourage sleep-filled nights.

Paolo was also stony-broke in his personal life, thanks to the deviousness of some Australian charlatan called Vivienne Taylor. A few weeks earlier, the blackmailer had threatened to reveal their one-off affair to his wife unless he gave her the dregs of his bank account. With no other choice, he was forced to comply with her demands.

Today, when one of the nurses approached him with a ridiculous plan, Paolo immediately said yes. Not because he was a big softie as Ludovico had thought, but because Riccardo Trentini had outstayed his welcome in Stella della Laguna by some thirty years. His pathetic insurance policy barely covered his breakfast.

'*Buona* idea! *Bravo!*'

And so it was agreed. Even though Riccardo—or Pádraig—was far from a suitable candidate to make such an arduous journey, Ludovico had just been given the go-ahead to organise a return to Ireland. There, the two super-centenarians would finally get the opportunity to meet under the sycamore tree and undo the terrible treachery that Mrs Keogh had committed over a hundred years earlier. Paolo wasn't too fussed about where precisely the pair ended up, so long as it meant that he had a free bed to sell at long last.

* * *

Sister Agatha had always given credit where it was due—and,

sometimes, even where it was not. For instance, she always gave two thumbs up every time Sister Ursula had presented a new piece of artwork. She even found some kind words to say when Sister de Lourdes, convinced that she was Estée Lauder, had painted her well-worn face with whatever makeup she could find before strutting around the convent, complete with orange skin, lipstick-stained teeth, and a figurative rod, fishing for compliments.

Fortunately, there was no need to lie to Stella della Laguna's staff, who deserved every kind word. They treated their guest of honour to the most delicious menu of food imaginable—but so much of it! While she prided herself in having a vigorous appetite, even dustbins had their limits. Sitting at the top of the dining room's large oak table, they placed course after course in front of her—from cured meats and olives to risotto and pasta, from sliced artichokes and roasted aubergines to grilled fish and steak. The staff waited eagerly for her verdict on every plate, meaning that she had no other option than to force the lot down her gob! From what she knew about the Italians, they were proud of their food—and for a good reason—so she wasn't willing to run the risk of insulting them by showing restraint with her mouthfuls.

After working her way through a mountainous portion of tiramisu, Sister Agatha conceded that tiredness—and bloatedness—had finally gotten the better of her. (They had earlier insisted that she stay with them at Stella della Laguna—an offer that the penny-pinching nun wasn't going to refuse.)

'Would you mind terribly if my bursting belly and I retire for the night?'

Earlier, there had been a suggestion from Ludovico that Sister Agatha might like to spend the night in Riccardo's bedroom, that an extra bed could have been brought in and placed next to him if she so desired, but the God-fearing kitchen porter had, thankfully, put the kibosh on that idea somewhat lively. Was Ludovico not aware that Sister Agatha had been married to the good Lord for a hundred years?

Even though she would have slept at the bottom of a well, the exhausted nun was relieved to hear that this room-sharing idea had gone no further. She had clocked that Riccardo had dreadful digestive troubles that reminded her of those recent, unpleasant roadworks outside the convent in Navan. Instead, the kind staff had arranged for Sister Agatha to get a good night's sleep in Signor Scarpa's office, where they placed a large, bumpy camping bed in front of his desk. (There was an avalanche of '*scuse*' made about a lack of available beds, thanks to their patients' frustratingly good genes.)

But Sister Agatha was more than happy with her temporary lodgings; given the week that was, she simply wanted to hightail it to the land of Nod and remain there for as long as possible.

'*Buona notte!*'

'*Dorma bene!*'

'*Sogni d'oro!*'

After these emotional goodbyes, Sister Agatha carelessly placed her fabulous new dress across a wooden chair, hastily deposited her teeth into a glass of water, then promptly crawled under the sheets and closed her eyes. Much to her dismay—and surprise—sleep would not come, and some twenty minutes later, Sister Agatha was still tossing and turning. She attempted to count sheep, but such was her irritation, those carefree woolly animals went from hopping over little wooden fences to becoming entrapped in reams of barbed wire—an image that didn't promote rest, she soon realised.

Sleep did not elude Sister Agatha because she was the victim of some troublesome indigestion like a particular patient down the hall. It was due to the kaleidoscopic thoughts whirling around her mind—and they were primarily guilt-related. Sister Agatha had come to Stella della Laguna that afternoon with one intention: to become the oldest person in the world. However, having been too taken by Venice's many charms to concoct a proper murderous plan ('If you'd witnessed the vistas over the lagoon, you'd have been a little distracted, too!'), she arrived unprepared.

The next thing she realised, her visit to the nursing home was assumed by those working here to have had an entirely different purpose altogether, leading her to receive the most extraordinary hospitality imaginable. And now, sprawled out on the fold-up bed, Sister Agatha was livid with herself for reciprocating their generosity by taking full advantage of their confusion. Simply put: Pádraig was not Riccardo, and Riccardo was not Pádraig.

Yes, various journalists discussed in great detail the uncertainty that clouded

Riccardo's early years. And yes, there was a striking resemblance between a younger Sister Agatha and his sculptures. And yes, she could easily have been the missing piece of the fantastic puzzle Ludovico had invented. But no, it was all just a remarkable coincidence, and she should have told them so. Instead, Sister Agatha had embraced the unexpected opportunity to recall her childhood romance with Pádraig and why an emerald ring hung from her rosary beads. Worst of all, she allowed them to believe that Riccardo was Pádraig, and now, the two sweethearts were being reunited at long last. It was a silly thing to have done, she realised—after all, Butsy Miller was now expected to love Riccardo and not smother him with one of his pillows.

Maybe her duplicity had sprung from her need to share her story at long last. Ever since Sister Agatha had discovered how Mrs Keogh had played such a hand in Butsy Miller's fate, she had chosen to keep it to herself. What was the point in dwelling on the past? She had followed a different path in life, and that was that. Then, today, a rare opportunity presented itself to give voice to that hugely important episode of her life—an episode that was instrumental in her making an improbable vow to be the oldest person in the world. And so, she nabbed it.

As she cast the blankets from her body—and cursed the inbuilt corset on her dress for having left her ribs fit only for the scrapheap—Sister Agatha wished she had not been so self-indulgent and had kept things to herself. It was a nonsensical, egotistical and unhelpful thing to have done. More importantly, it was certainly not going to see her ascend that final step on the podium. Before she could continue with her self-flagellation, a gentle knock came on the door.

'Yes?' she called out after returning her false teeth to their rightful position.

'Might I come in for *un secondo, Sorella*?'

Before Sister Agatha could answer, Ludovico was sitting on the bed, about to burst with excitement.

'I have a big surprise for you,' he whispered, his voice filled with dramatic and conspiratorial tones. 'I didn't want to say anything in front of the others because, well, selfishly, I wanted your reaction all for myself!'

Sister Agatha had hoped that the day would not get any more difficult; it seemed that her effervescent friend seated in front of her had other ideas.

'I have agreed on everything with Signor Scarpa, and I have just made all the other necessary arrangements online.'

When he revealed the ins and outs of his big scheme, Sister Agatha could hardly believe her ears. Maybe she was, after all, in a dream-like state, and the words being unleashed from Ludovico's mouth were just a figment of her imagination.

'Could you repeat that once again, my dear?'

According to Ludovico, she and Riccardo were to be escorted from Venice to Ireland first thing in the morning and then whisked away to that old sycamore tree in Kilberry where, after all these years, Butsy Miller and Pádraig Keogh would finally get to meet.

'I don't—' Sister Agatha tried to argue, but before she could even begin to explain how ridiculous the idea was, the nurse kissed her on the cheek, then rushed towards the door. Of course, Sister Agatha realised that it was a beautiful gesture—and she genuinely hated to disappoint this adorable, if somewhat unhinged, teddy bear of a man—but she only had three days remaining to live. If she had to play the reluctant hostess to Riccardo, under constant surveillance, how on earth would she kill him? She only had herself to blame for this sorry mess!

Why didn't you come prepared?

Sister Agatha decided that she must come clean, cut her losses, and flee back to the convent, content that she had almost achieved her vow.

'Ludovico, I have been somewhat loose with the truth, and I—'

'By the way,' the nurse interrupted. 'Because of Riccardo's—I mean Pádraig's—condition, the journey will probably mean that he will die as soon as we arrive at the tree in Kilberry. But I think that's what he would have wanted: to slip away in the arms of the love of his life, don't you?'

Without so much as a bat of the eyelids, Sister Agatha turned to Ludovico and nodded piously. 'I couldn't have put it better myself.'

EIGHTEEN

In front of the Aer Lingus gate in Venice's Marco Polo Airport, Sister Agatha and Riccardo sat together, although the latter could barely keep vertical, despite being propped up in a wheelchair by a strap. Behind them stood Ludovico—not that a passer-by would have been able to tell; he was practically hidden underneath the mounds of bags, medication and the other essentials needed for the ambitious journey. Since leaving Stella della Laguna, his incredible romanticism had gone to war with the sliver of realism he possessed. The bumpy, hour-long journey to the airport aboard the *Alilaguna* ferry had clarified that Riccardo barely had the strength to leave his bedroom, let alone venture back to his beloved Navan.

Am I a fool? Ludovico asked himself repeatedly throughout the morning.

This wasn't the first time he had allowed his heart to rule his head, and if past experiences were anything to go by, the payoffs did not always prove successful. Once, in the middle of a busy shift, he had interrupted a teenager ransacking the supply room. When the unexpected visitor explained that the medication bulging in his pockets was for his sick niece, not only did Ludovico overlook the fact that the chap bore all the hallmarks of a homeless heroin addict, but he also gave him the loan of his car to bring the young child—who had just been fabricated at that very moment—to the hospital.

When Ludovico read an article on the front page of *Il Gazzettino* the following day, which detailed a bank robbery in the nearby city of Mestre, his suspicions were aroused. What's more, the facial composite that accompanied the report looked uncomfortably familiar—as did the description of the red Fiat that facilitated the successful heist. It took a good lawyer and numerous trips to the local carabinieri to convince authorities that the gullible and harmless nurse had no part in the crime.

Today, as he looked at Sister Agatha wiping away unsightly drool from the mouth of her soul mate—now sleeping on her shoulder—Ludovico knew that this modern-day Romeo and Juliet were destined to be together under that sycamore tree. Many would describe this journey as dangerous, but it was also essential, he now reminded himself.

Whatever the cost.

Some of Ludovico's initial fears were abated thanks to the amiable airline staff.

'What an honour it is for us to have you on board,' Sinéad, the flight purser, declared, ushering the pair onto the plane ahead of everyone else. She promised to treat the elderly couple like two important heads of state—no less than what they deserved, Ludovico felt.

Speaking of all things old, a tatty suitcase belonging to his late grandfather lived under Ludovico's bed. Within it, the nurse stashed any decoration related to *amore*. When Stella della Laguna didn't require his services, Ludovico went from church to church all over Venice, participating in strangers' wedding celebrations. After showering them with confetti and his best wishes, he would ransack the church and swipe all of the adornments the bride and groom used to mark their big day. From cut-out hearts, balloons and streamers to confetti, posters and banners—if it were red, pink or sparkly and alluded to love in any way, he placed it into his grandfather's *valigia*, convinced that they would be put to good use one day. Today was that day. Deciding to take full advantage of her hospitality, he asked Sinéad for permission to transform the lovebirds' seats into something more worthy of their fantastic story.

'Leave it with me—I'll see what I can do!' his new ally told him.

As Sinéad disappeared to chat with the pilot, Ludovico, confident that his thoughtful idea would receive the green light, wasted no time getting his many trinkets out of the suitcase. He scattered nearly a paper mill worth of confetti over, under and around the pair, before adorning Sister Agatha's hair and Riccardo's buttonholes with a selection of plastic roses.

'Don't you both look only *magnifici*!' he praised after completing his decorating.

Just as he was about to pop open some streamers, Sinéad returned with the unfortunate news that while the pilot possessed the most beautiful cheekbones in Europe, he also had a heart of stone.

'On account of stringent security regulations, he said flourishes were forbidden,' she recounted. '"What if there's an emergency landing?" blah, blah, blah.'

'But…' Ludovico argued feebly. '*Allora*—fine!'

He begrudgingly gathered up all of the enchanting second-hand wedding favours and returned them to his grandfather's suitcase.

The pilot has clearly never experienced true love, he lamented, stowing the decorations in the overhead locker. He then sat beside the couple, taking comfort in the fact that, one day, their beautiful love story would be celebrated the world over—regardless of any bothersome security rules or pernickety pilots. Maybe a film would be made of their romance, which could then premiere at the Venice Film Festival—oh, how glorious that would be! And instead of being squashed by other film fans, as had been the case throughout the years, Ludovico would be walking the red carpet himself—the star of the show! Thoroughly enjoying the fantasy, the nurse placed his own head on Sister Agatha's free shoulder and said a little prayer.

Nel nome del Padre, del Figlio e dello Spirito Santo.

Ludovico had refused to give up hope that Stella della Laguna would, one day, receive a special visitor, despite what several staff members maintained. And now that the Irish nun had arrived to reclaim what was rightfully hers, the story transpired to be even more magical than he could have ever imagined.

Grazie, mio Dio. Grazie for making Butsy Miller—or Sister Agatha, as you also know her—such a strong, honest and kind-hearted person. If only there were more of her in the world.

He quickly blessed himself, then, inspired by the pair beside him, rested his eyes for a brief moment. After the excitement of the past twenty-four hours, nobody would begrudge the guy a little nap.

Ludovico awoke from his nap somewhere over France, desperately needing a strong espresso. Having missed the refreshments trolley during its initial round, he made his way to the crew rest. While waiting for his beverage, he couldn't help but give Sinéad the complete A-to-Z on Butsy Miller and Pádraig Keogh's heart-warming story and how, following all those years, they had finally been reunited.

'Aren't they a real marvel? They don't make them like that anymore,' the air hostess replied, genuinely captivated by what she had just heard—and almost scalding herself in the process.

Just as Ludovico returned to his seat, a strong cup of coffee in hand, an announcement boomed across the tannoy.

'Ladies and gentlemen, will you give me your attention for a second?' Sinéad said. 'We have two extraordinary passengers on board our flight this morning, and if anyone needs a pick-me-up story, listen closely!'

There followed a lively retelling of the lives of Butsy and Pádraig, with Sinéad happily adding legs to the story for good measure. For example, she heavily implied that Mr Keogh's untimely death—when Pádraig was just ten years of age—lay at the hands of the man's evil wife. And the reason why her seven daughters were overweight was that Mrs Keogh, jealous of their youth, had force-fed them 'any auld schlop' to diminish their confidence and boost her own. (She later regretted this tactic, finding it impossible to flog them off to any bachelor, eligible or otherwise). While those details were her own invention, Sinéad probably hypothesised correctly on both counts.

When the epic tale had been brought up to date, a euphoric round of applause sounded, with almost enough tears shed to cause an early descent. Gayle, a middle-aged lady from Offaly, returning to Ireland following a few weeks away from her oafish husband, decided there and then to finally listen to her instinct and accept that her marriage was over. The story of Butsy and Pádraig was true love; the story of Gayle and Micheál O'Shaughnessy was a sham—a marriage of convenience because she had been unfortunate to become pregnant at just nineteen. Yes, as soon as the fifty-seven-year-old returned home to Birr, she vowed to send the swine and his dirty fingernails packing.

When some of the passengers approached Sister Agatha and Riccardo to pass on their admiration and congratulations, they were disappointed to see that the duo remained deep in slumber, though such a state was understandable, they agreed, given their vintage. Ludovico, still somewhat indignant that his suitcase full of magic gathered dust in the overhead locker, now felt encouraged by the support from those around him and asked Sinéad to petition the pilot for permission one more time.

'Leave it with me!' Sinéad told him.

But her efforts fell short, as the pilot had little interest in such revelry and threatened to divert the plane if his passengers didn't settle down. (Despite his chiselled jawline, Captain Morris had never enjoyed much luck with the ladies and, as such, sported a bitter lip when discussing matters of the heart.)

After that, the flight returned to its more conventional, humdrum tempo, and as soon as the caffeine focused him, Ludovico decided not to try the patience of the pilot again. He noticed Riccardo's breathing was becoming increasingly laboured, a reminder that time was not on their side. The last thing anyone needed was a diversion to some airport in Luxembourg or Belgium. No, there would be plenty of time to liberate the contents of his suitcase once they had made their way to Kilberry, he decided. Until then, he would just relax and enjoy the rest of the flight.

Better again, why not let his imagination run wild and visualise the possible suits or tuxedos that the world's leading fashionistas would design for him for the Venice Film Festival première of the upcoming Butsy and Pádraig biopic, *You Don't Know What You've Got Till It's Gondola*?

When the plane descended into Dublin just before midday, it emerged that Sinéad and the other crew members had phoned ahead to organise a guard of honour for the two sweethearts. But being an age when it wasn't just infections that went viral, the news spread, and an army of camera crews and photographers waited fervently at Dublin Airport, enchanted by the tale that currently enjoyed robust discussion across every social media outlet around the globe.

At the arrivals' hall, the relentless clatter of click, click, click greeted the triumphant contingent, which consisted of Sister Agatha, Riccardo, Ludovico and the entire Aer Lingus crew (one grumpy pilot aside)—not to mention two hundred passengers who walked, procession-like, behind them. When Sister Agatha worked out the reason behind the commotion, a smile crept onto her face. While her fifteen minutes of fame had arrived about an hour too early (the turbulence-free flight might not have signalled the death knell for Riccardo, but the potholes on the back roads of County Meath would surely do the trick), she wasn't one to look a gift-horse in the mouth. She threw herself into the moment with admirable gusto, waving and smiling beatifically at the world's media. She gave herself a figurative pat on the back for having the wisdom to enjoy some early morning sunshine in Venice. As a result, Sister Agatha's sun-kissed complexion glowed just as brightly as her halcyon days—something that the press and her adoring public were sure to appreciate.

On the other hand, Riccardo remained almost catatonic throughout the hullabaloo—the only sign of life was the continuous drooling and occasional grumble of the belly. The questions from the media came ad infinitum.

'How does it feel being reunited after all these years?'

'Did he still recognise you, Sister Agatha?'

'Are you going to defect from the convent and get married?'

'Will you take his name or remain Butsy Miller?'

Convinced that a picture was worth a thousand words, Sister Agatha remained tight-lipped and instead took centre stage, throwing her arms around Riccardo, even giving him a little kiss on the cheek—much to the delight of all around them. A complete natural in front of the camera and her many fans, Sister Agatha fancied that if she hadn't followed a life of prayer, she could easily have given Ava Gardner a run for her money in Hollywood.

The VIP treatment continued outside the building. While Sister Agatha might have slummed it on a bus from Navan to the airport a week earlier, now, a shiny, top-of-the-range BMW awaited her.

What rotten luck that Doctor McManus' prognosis was so grim—I could get used to this treatment, she thought, accepting a bouquet of roses from a young schoolgirl.

A beaming Paul, her loyal taxi driver, assisted her and the others into the flashy car, which contained, amongst other things, the largest box of chocolates Sister Agatha had ever seen.

'This is no more than you deserve!' Paul whispered to the golden girl.

'I couldn't have put it better myself!' she replied, making light work of the crème caramels.

NINETEEN

THE IRISH INDEPENDENT, 15 MARCH 2016

Without a shadow of a doubt, this is a love story that trumps all others. Forget Elizabeth and Richard, Wallis and Edward or John and Oko. The heart-warming tale of an Irish nun who travelled at the tender age of 118 to three continents to find her childhood sweetheart is one that all others will be compared against in the future.

A series of obstacles prevented their courtship from flourishing in the early part of the 20th century, but foolish is the person who underestimates the power of love because a mind-blowing 100 years later, they were reunited in the suitably romantic Italian city of Venice.

Sister Agatha, born Butsy Miller, and Riccardo Trentini, born Pádraig Keogh, pursued significantly different lives in the intervening years. One spent her days devoted to God, the other to his art. But one thing they shared in common was a healthy heart because, apart from all else, these valentines are the two oldest people in the world, with Pádraig having the slight edge, being 121 years of age.

The pair is now set to return to their beloved Kilberry, where they will spend the remainder of their days together. When interviewed at Dublin Airport earlier this afternoon following their return from Venice, Sister Agatha was too busy fussing over her darling Pádraig to answer questions, but his nurse, Ludovico Bianchi, who was instrumental in bringing the two lovebirds home to Ireland, spoke of their immediate plans.

159

'We are going to the large sycamore tree that plays an enormous role in their story,' he revealed. 'They just want to sit there for a few minutes, together. After that, who knows?'

In an age where relationships rise and fall in the blink of an eye, Butsy Miller and Pádraig Keogh perfectly exemplify that true love is eternal.

* * *

The sycamore tree had seen much over the years, but nothing quite like the spectacle it was witnessing today. Thousands of well-wishers stood alongside an endless stream of reporters, weighed down by their cameras, microphones and laptops. While their editors usually encouraged more substantial news items, they knew that few could resist a good old-fashioned love story like this. The crowds kept growing, and when they weren't fighting each other to get the best view, they were checking their watches as the duo was expected to arrive any minute now. And when they weren't timekeeping, they were praying that the weather would hold and that those ominous clouds hovering in the distance would remain on their best behaviour.

Local businesses didn't miss a trick and impressively found opportunities to showcase their wares. A local tannery, Hell for Leather, had gone hell for leather to produce last-minute cloaks for the lovers; wet or dry, spring weather could be perilous, particularly for those of a certain age. A nearby woollen mill had made a couple of cosy hats and mittens, while every café, pub and restaurant had sent their chefs into a frenzy by ordering them to rustle up food fit for such a regal reunion.

The Mother Superior and the other nuns from the Order of Saint Aloysius had also dashed to the tree, still battling the confusion and embarrassment that nobody had been aware that Sister Agatha had even left the country. (Didn't Sister Fidelma mention that she was visiting some non-existent in-law for a couple of days?) To drown out any wicked whispers of negligence, Sister Veronica had dragged the youngsters out of the school, and even though they had barely sung a note in their lives, the four-year-olds were expected to perform like the Vienna Boys' Choir.

(When the Mother Superior soon discovers the whopping million euro just lodged into the convent's bank, the Order will be able to send for those famed Austrian crooners themselves.)

Members of the parish had ensured that both the sycamore tree and surrounding grass looked neat and tidy. Lawnmowers, shears and trimmers, which weren't due to make an appearance for another few days, had been put to great use. Even though the day was bright, lanterns and fairy lights were hoisted up onto the branches while a cream, three-seater couch was wrenched out of Mrs Smith's sitting room for the occasion. If the world's eyes were on Kilberry, locals were determined that their charming community would be shown off in the best possible light. (They even wore their Sunday Bests—and it was only Tuesday!)

At a quarter past three, the black BMW was said to have been spotted, although most people waited to see the car with their own eyes because Charlie, the boy who trumpeted its arrival, was a notorious liar. (He recently claimed that he had been the victim of a UFO abduction and taken to a far-off planet, where he was forced to perform every winning Eurovision song since the contest started. Johnny Logan and Dana were the leader's favourites, Charlie had informed the community on return.) This time, Charlie was actually telling the truth, and when a line of cars, headed by Sister Agatha and Riccardo, pulled into the church car park, thunderous applause followed, one usually reserved for the All-Ireland Football Final.

'There's hope for us all,' muttered Gerry Donnelly, a seventy-year-old bachelor, fed up with having to cook for one every night.

And that emerged to be the consensus—not just in County Meath, but in the four corners of the globe: Life had no Best Before.

* * *

Mario Gentili, the host of a top-rated Italian radio show, *Lo Show di Mario Gentili*, prided himself on being the personification of enthusiasm. Whenever there was an opening to attend, the DJ was there—cutting the ribbon, if required. Whenever there was a birthday in the studios, the sixty-six-year-old was there—belting out '*Tanti Auguri a Tè*', if required. And whenever there was the need to raise money for a good cause, Mario was in the midst of it—spearheading the fundraising, if required.

When he received a press release for a campaign that aimed to prevent the demolition of a centuries-old water mill in Tuscany, Mario was the first to sign up. He even suggested a suitable event, sure to bring attention to the cause: a boxing tournament.

'Let's show them they will have to knock us down before they knock the water mill down!'

Always game for an exciting challenge, Mario also proposed taking on one of Italy's finest boxers—an Olympic medallist at that—in the televised charity match. While most people would baulk at going into a ring with a world-class heavyweight half their age, Mario Gentili was not remotely fazed by the task ahead. He believed that it would take more than a few punches to knock him out—after all, being the only surviving blood relative of Riccardo Trentini, the oldest man in the world, meant that he had remarkable genes.

While their actual connection was nothing to shout about (third cousins twice removed, or something along those lines), the radio star was the one person who knew that Riccardo wasn't the Pádraig Keogh the world now believed him to be. That is to say, he was the only person able to put an end to Sister Agatha's charade.

During a private training session with his feisty coach, Elisabetta—who was highly impressed by her protegee's robustness, despite his years—Mario was drawn to a news report on the television. An interview from Dublin Airport featured some flamboyant nurse who, all-a-flutter, described how fate (and a wretched mother) had initially kept a nun and Mario's third cousin twice removed (or something like that) apart but, ultimately, had brought them together again.

'Cosa? Riccardo grew up in an orphanage after his mother died of pneumonia!' Mario told Elisabetta, who was too preoccupied with jabbing him in the stomach to hear what he was saying. (There was also a pesky gum shield lodged firmly in his mouth with which he had to contend.)

162

'I must ring the network and tell them *la verità*!' he mumbled, saliva flying everywhere.

But Mario never received the opportunity to make any such call because his trainer, full of vim and vigour on that particular day (a dress she had ordered online had just arrived, and it was even nicer than she had hoped!), proved to be a little too enthusiastic with her punches. As such, a distracted Mario Gentili fell backwards and knocked his head against one of the steel posts, rendering him unconscious.

Petrified that she would be held accountable (and never get an opportunity to wear her lovely new dress), Elisabetta panicked and ran for the hills where she lived in a modest log cabin. The poor man's near-lifeless body wasn't discovered until the following morning after failing to turn up for *Lo Show di Mario Gentili*.

Mario's vibrant life suddenly ground to a temporary halt. Unlike the water mill, which was offered a last-minute reprieve by some philanthropic businessman and eventually turned into a swanky restaurant. If only the broadcaster didn't have to spend the following six months in the hospital battling, amongst other things, complete memory loss, he would have loved to have attended the restaurant's glamorous opening.

* * *

On the journey to Kilberry, a makeup artist and stylist sponsored by one of the commercial television networks hopped into the BMW and gave Sister Agatha a drastic transformation. Layers of makeup were caked onto her face while her thinning hair received a boost.

'If this journey doesn't kill Pádraig, the fumes from the hairspray probably will,' Ludovico joked in a wonderfully passive-aggressive manner.

When Sister Agatha caught a glimpse of herself in the mirror, she was nicely impressed; if only the convent hadn't shunned such embellishments over the years, she would surely have had long queues of admirers lining up! Riccardo was left just the way he was. After the finishing touches had been applied, Sister Agatha stepped out of the car, successfully channelling the spirit of some silver-screen starlet. Not even the pontiff himself could identify with the adulation this luminary currently received from the home crowd.

'We love you guys!'

'You're our heroine, Sister Agatha!'

'Can you kiss my baby's head, Pádraig?'

Over the past week, Sister Agatha hadn't thought twice about indulging in spontaneity and decided that now wasn't an appropriate time to change her ways. So, disregarding the agreed itinerary, she broke away from the group and greeted the many supporters whose love and warmth for Butsy Miller and Pádraig Keogh were infectious. Ludovico capitalised on Sister Agatha's deviation by running towards the tree and adorning it with the contents of his grandfather's valigia. He might have been held to ransom by health-and-safety restrictions on the plane journey over, but now he was free to decorate as he pleased.

Meanwhile, Sister Agatha, completely swept away by the occasion, relished signing one autograph after the other for her legion of admirers.

'Is that Hillary with one 'l' or two?'

Doctor McManus, standing beside Doreen Cooney and her new cat, received the cold shoulder—if he'd had his way, Sister Agatha wouldn't have even left his surgery, let alone sailed the Seven Seas! But before any heated words could be exchanged between the pair, Ludovico returned, demanding that Sister Agatha focus on why they were all there in the first place.

'And don't forget, Sister—time isn't on our side!' he whispered conspiratorially.

Reluctantly, the nun tore herself away from the merry mob and readied herself to assist her wheelchair-bound sidekick across the field to the tree that had been so integral to the original story of Butsy and Pádraig. Before the first step could be taken, a magazine editor, who was due to conduct an exclusive interview with the couple later that day, stood in front of them, his face alive with another exciting idea.

'Why don't you get rid of his wheelchair and try to walk over to the tree together?'

Ludovico gasped. 'He will never make it! You do realise that he is a hundred-and-twenty-one years of age?'

The editor shrugged. 'Give it a try.'

'Absolutely not!' Ludovico protested but secretly thought it would be the most adorable end to their story (and the perfect final sequence for *You Don't Know What You've Got Till It's Gondola*).

'I think it's a splendid idea,' Sister Agatha interjected, carefully lifting Riccardo from the wheelchair. She draped his arm around her shoulder and took one final deep breath.

'Are you sure this is a good idea?' Ludovico asked one last time.

'I will be given all the strength and support I need from the goodwill of these generous and kind people,' Sister Agatha reassured him.

Before the duo could embark on their monumental journey across the car park towards the sycamore tree, Ludovico couldn't resist giving them one last passionate embrace (before dousing them in blasted glitter and confetti).

'Break a leg!' he said, tears streaming down his flushed cheeks.

Sister Agatha hoped that she wouldn't have to inflict any such damage on her new acquaintance's frail body. No, if any assault were to occur, she prayed it would just be Riccardo kicking the proverbial bucket.

* * *

At Stella della Laguna, a day wouldn't pass for Riccardo Trentini without being henpecked by one of the nurses who, for an unknown reason, seemed convinced that the sculptor was a real-life character from some romantic motion picture or shoddy three-act opera. His near-fossilised body gave the impression that he wasn't receptive to the world around him; unfortunately, he gauged quite a bit of what went on, which, for the most part, was this astonishingly silly nurse waxing lyrical about a supposed melodrama in which Riccardo assumed the leading role. Of course, matters of the heart had played a considerable part in the life of Signor Trentini—he was a libidinous Italian, after all—but these previous and thrilling encounters with physical intimacy, often with his models, never lasted longer than a satisfying tumble and a fumble.

For the sculptor, the best aspect of Stella della Laguna was that his modest bedroom had been transformed into a make-shift gallery. The work that occupied the space never ceased to energise and fuel him, allowing his creaky mind to remain engaged. Samson had famously found his strength in his hair—for Riccardo, it was in his art. Even though many of his companions at Stella della Laguna had tired of being force-fed another grim breakfast on earth, opting to dine with the gods in Heaven instead, Riccardo, surrounded by his work, persevered. This outlook recently changed. After catching snippets of a conversation about how the remaining four pieces of his collections were to be auctioned off to foot his bill, at long last, he wanted out. There was little point in living without his work beside him—empowering him to battle on.

Yes, before they wrapped up his sculptures and carted them off to their new homes, the artist felt that there was no better time than now to pull the curtains down on his extraordinarily long and, for the most part, successful life.

Riccardo never feared death. On the contrary, he saw it as a beautiful transitional process and not the conclusion many believed. What he would describe as bleak and dark and lifeless was an existence without his sculptures around him. Samson had crumbled when Delilah chopped off his mane, and now that the owner of Stella della Laguna was taking his lead from that hair-cutting, duplicitous biblical figure, Riccardo wanted to relinquish life. Yes, he was certain that it was time to give up the ghost, once and for all. But, according to the doctors, his body continued to enjoy good rude health—so, what was there to do? Riccardo had often prayed during his long life, but he never wanted them to be answered more than now.

And then, a strange Irish nun suddenly appeared.

* * *

Under the watchful eye of the world, Sister Agatha and Riccardo set off on their momentous journey. Not since the days of Neil

Armstrong and Buzz Aldrin sauntering across the moon's surface had the simple act of walking received such glory and acclaim. One step at a time became the duo's mantra, and, sure enough, they started to make real progress. For a moment, it appeared as if the impossible undertaking might prove possible—that was until the light of one of the camera bulbs almost blinded Sister Agatha, resulting in her stumbling over a stone, which, in turn, led them both to crash onto the ground beneath them. The world gasped but none more so than Ludovico, who valiantly ignored several mini-strokes and raced to his charges, helping them back to their feet.

'*Mamma mia!* I knew I shouldn't have—'

'We've come this far—we can't stop now,' Sister Agatha insisted, dusting herself off. 'We'll make it; I know we will.'

With Sister Fidelma busy in the crowd taking bets as to whether this would be the case, Sister Agatha took a deep breath and, arms linked with her sidekick, ploughed on towards what was now the world's most famous tree. Inch by inch, they moved closer to their final destination, and when it looked as if the task at hand would prove impossible, the roars of encouragement intensified. (Sister Fidelma was particularly in fine voice—she had a thousand euro on a positive outcome.)

When the pair stood just metres away from the tree—with Mrs Smith's inviting couch underneath—a spontaneous countdown commenced.

'Ten! Nine! Eight!'

Completely fagged, Sister Agatha reminded herself that she had never been one to admit defeat and that she certainly must not start that carry-on now.

Didn't you survive the Sahara sun? Escape maniacal gunmen in Chicago? Was it not you who freed yourself from that deranged spy in Warsaw? You've got it in you; I know you have!

And on they went.

'Seven! Six!' chanted the crowd.

Even though the remaining energy in her reserves was now completely depleted, Sister Agatha refused to give up—just three more steps was all that was needed.

You have clocked up thousands upon thousands of miles over the week. All you now require are just a few more steps!

And on they went.

'Five! Four!'

With a solitary step left, the couple was so close and yet so far—Sister Agatha could barely hold herself upright, let alone support Riccardo's surprisingly heavy weight. In desperate need of motivation, the nun fished the emerald ring out from under her dress—a piece of jewellery that she had kept near her heart for over a century. She gripped it so tightly, it was a wonder she didn't go the route of Padre Pio and stigmatise herself.

I'm doing this for you, Pádraig, she whispered to it. You've got to help me—don't abandon me again, do you hear?

She then brazenly turned to Riccardo for support, only to find his head drooping in front of him and on the verge of dislodging itself from the rest of his body.

And that was the moment when Sister Agatha finally realised what she was doing. She was killing a sweet man who had humbly spent his life inspiring people through his art—all so that she could fulfil the improbable vow that she had made some fifty years earlier. Before her, Sister Agatha saw the most vulnerable little soul in the entire universe. Before her, she saw innocence being exploited.

What are you doing, you wicked, depraved girl? she silently screamed at herself, releasing her hold of the emerald ring.

As the errors of her ways became even more apparent, the roars from the crowds only heightened, now reaching a fever pitch. Their cries of support could have been heard in Tunisia, America, Poland and Italy. A single step was all that was needed for Sister Agatha to reach that infernal sycamore and claim her prize, but, at the final hurdle, she decided to do something that she had never done in her entire life: throw in the towel. As much as she would like to think otherwise, Sister Agatha was not cut out for this murdering lark.

You still have time to make amends.

That was when something rather incredible occurred. As if there hadn't been enough miracles taking place over the past number of days, for the first time in over thirty years, Riccardo's eyes fully opened and came to life. With the speed of a tortoise, he raised his head and turned to Sister Agatha.

'*Tre, due, uno!*' he mumbled.

And just like that, with perspiration springing from every pore, Riccardo lugged Sister Agatha one step forward before slumping onto Mrs Smith's beautiful cream couch. The dynamic duo had made it! Absolute hysterics followed from the onlookers and media. Around the globe, suckers for happy endings were glued to their television screens and computers. Even some of the world's most hardened leaders and politicians had taken time out from passing brown envelopes to each other to watch history being made. Riccardo clasped Sister Agatha's hands and let his head fall on her shoulder.

'*Grazie*,' he muttered in a barely audible manner. Although she wasn't altogether confident that she fully understood what he meant, Sister Agatha suspected that Riccardo had had his fill of this life and was eager to be reunited with his chisel and marble in the next.

A moment's privacy was all the pair was afforded. As the applause died down, so too did Riccardo Trentini. The world's oldest person released a soft groan and took his last breath. The crowd collectively gasped, moving from joy to despair in the blink of an eye. Their attention quickly turned to Sister Agatha to see what form her sorrowful reaction might take. While there were no hard-and-fast rules to grief, some eagle-eyed observers were surprised to detect a smile etched across Butsy Miller's face.

TWENTY

The final week of June 1932 was one that Ireland would never forget. A flurry of excitement enveloped Dublin due to the arrival of the thirty-first International Eucharistic Congress. The city promised to pull out all the stops to ensure that this event would be the envy of the world. A fleet of ocean liners had even gathered along Sir John Rogerson's Quay, acting as floating hotels to meet the demand for accommodation from the country's three million Catholics who had descended upon the capital for this auspicious occasion.

While daily prayer was commonplace in the country at that time, who or what they were being said for often varied: a sick relative, an end to poverty, a wayward husband. That summer, there was only one reason why Irish people were on their hands and knees: to beg the Lord above that the rain would stay away. They could handle wind or a sky covered in clouds, but rain just wouldn't do. Think of all the cardinals and archbishops in their lovely regalia—and what a disaster it would be if they got wet! And it seemed that God took pity on them because their prayers were answered, and the weather held out, much to the delight of everyone.

On the final day of the five-day event, a mass took place in the Phoenix Park, and a quarter of the country's population was present, including a much younger Sister Agatha, who had never seen anything quite so magnificent in all her life. The celebrations proved too fantastic and overwhelming for the thirty-four-year-old country girl, and she was forced to slip away from the crowd to catch her breath.

Not knowing the city's layout, Sister Agatha found herself strolling in the direction of Kilmainham Gaol, the prison where some of Ireland's most prolific freedom fighters had been incarcerated just sixteen years earlier. She happened upon a bench nearby and sat down. After a minute, probably the only other person who had dodged the mass sat beside her. With him stood a pram, although inside, instead of a sleeping baby, there was a bounty of religious paraphernalia and accoutrements—rosary beads, bibles, crosses, candles and pictures. If ever there were a day to make a few pence selling your God-worshipping wares, Sister Agatha mused, it was today. Opening a battered leather pouch, the seller rolled a cigarette. Who could begrudge the man a small moment of relief amidst a busy day of wheeling and dealing?

Readying herself to re-join her fellow nuns at the Phoenix Park, Sister Agatha noticed that the man's hands had been scorched. She then turned her attention to his face, saddened to see that, beneath his tweed cap and bushy beard, his face was also besmirched with scars.

'I don't suppose I could trouble you for a light?' he asked, his voice soft, familiar.

'I'm afraid I don't smoke,' she answered.

'Not to worry, I shouldn't either anyway.'

After returning his tobacco pouch to his pocket, the two strangers sat in silence. Or were they strangers, Sister Agatha asked herself—she had this strong hunch that they had met before. While she knew that common decency deemed it vulgar to stare at somebody, Sister Agatha couldn't resist and, without apology, she gave etiquette short shrift. The man's facial hair, coupled with his extensive scarring, made it difficult for her to study his features properly, but when her new companion turned and smiled at her, Sister Agatha's now racing heart started to pulverise the walls of her chest.

It couldn't be, could it?

Ever since he had failed to show up that morning under the old sycamore tree, Sister Agatha had whiled away the hours, wondering whatever had happened to Pádraig Keogh. Did he still call Ireland home? Had he fallen in love again? What did he look like now? But she doubted that she would receive answers to these questions. Until now.

'I'm sorry, would you mind if I asked you your name?'

'Are you going to convert me?' he joked.

'No, of course not! You just remind me of someone I used to know.'

'Eamonn,' he said, outstretching her hand. 'And you?'

'Sister Agatha. Pleased to meet you.'

It was the exact second that their hands touched that Sister Agatha knew for sure.

'I suspect that Eamonn isn't the name your parents gave you at birth—sure it isn't, *Pádraig Keogh*?'

On hearing these words, Eamonn sat rooted to the spot, stupefied. It had been over seventeen years since anyone had called him by that name.

'Butsy, is that you?'

And that was how the reunion of the two old flames went.

In his modest lodgings, Pádraig—or Eamonn, as he had been calling himself since leaving County Meath in a bid to start anew—invited Sister Agatha to take a seat.

'Please excuse the mess—I wasn't expecting visitors today.'

The flat, while the size of a shoe rather than a shoebox, was one of the tidiest spaces she had ever seen, which was saying something considering she lived in an immaculately clean convent. Proving to have a talent for interior design, Pádraig had transformed the Rathmines flat into something she would have expected to see in the Gresham Hotel.

'It is beautiful,' Sister Agatha lauded, combing the space and looking for a few possible ideas to bring back to the convent.

Pádraig fished out a couple of bottles of ale from a press and offered one to his guest. While the convent frowned upon alcohol consumption—unless its main ingredient was the blood of Christ—Sister Agatha decided to ignore the strict rules that had shaped her life so far.

'I'll just have a drop,' she said, aware that such an ambitious promise had been the undoing of many a person over the years.

Bottles in hand, the pair sat on the couch and, for several moments, they remained silent, unsure of what to say.

'The Battle of Passchendaele in October 1917,' Pádraig finally announced—a couple of swigs of Beverwycks giving him a little Dutch courage.

'I'm sorry?'

'The burns—I'm sure you're wondering.'

In truth, Sister Agatha couldn't think of anything else but didn't know how to broach the subject.

'The Great War. Not knowing what else to do, I signed up to the army after....'

'After you reneged on your promise and humiliated me in front of the whole village?'

She gasped at her candour—alcohol was the devil's work, she soon realised.

'What—reneged? Good heavens, no! Is that what you think I did?'

'Well, wasn't it?' she replied, unable to keep her loose tongue under control.

For the next hour or so, Pádraig went into painful detail about his deceptive and scheming mother and the extraordinary charade she had conjured up, all so that the engagement would run aground.

'And you never received any of my correspondences?'

Dumbfounded by what she had just heard, Sister Agatha shook her head.

'Did you think I would abandon you like that?' he asked.

She wasn't sure if it were the effects of the alcohol or the news she had just received, but suddenly, Sister Agatha felt quite light-headed. Her heart broke all over again—not for herself and what had been stolen from her by the reprehensible Mrs Keogh—but for Pádraig's current existence. Grappling with poverty, solitude and the brutal loss of a once angelic appearance, his life had been completely and utterly destroyed.

'I have been told time and time again at the convent that God works in mysterious ways,' she meditated. 'But how can He justify making your life so difficult and lonely?'

'Lonely?' he probed. 'Why do you think I'm lonely?'

Before he could receive an answer, the door burst open and in ran a young and beautiful sallow-skinned girl, followed by a smiling, curly-haired woman, shopping bags in hand.

'Daddy!'

The girl jumped into Pádraig's arms, and as he embraced her, it appeared to Sister Agatha that all of his facial disfigurements had faded away. This warm, domestic scene enlivened the young nun; loneliness had not, thankfully, bullied its way into her old flame's life. It appeared that God does work in mysterious ways, she concluded.

Throughout the afternoon, Sister Agatha received the warmest of welcomes from the little family of three. She learned that Pádraig—or Eamonn—met his dear wife, a nurse, fifteen years previously while recovering from his injuries. She also discovered that little Margaret claimed an impressive six and a half years— and, more importantly, in four months, the youngster would become a big sister. Sister Agatha's former swain had realised his potential, becoming the man she knew he could be.

'Look at the hour!' the nun exclaimed when she realised that it was fast approaching five o'clock. She desperately needed to return to the Phoenix Park before the bus departed without her. (Not to mention finding a minute to pick up a sandwich along the way to soak up all of the beer that was making merry in her stomach).

'Please, let's remain in each other's lives,' Pádraig said, walking her out. 'Good friends are hard to come by. I lost you once, Butsy Miller; I don't want to lose you again.'

Sister Agatha threw her arms around Pádraig and held him close for a few heavenly moments. When they released each other, she removed the emerald ring from under her habit.

'I never lost you, Pádraig—and don't plan on doing so now.'

* * *

Over the following years, Sister Agatha kept her word and maintained a constant correspondence with her former partner-in-crime through letter-writing or, in later years, midnight phone calls. Sometimes, they would simply share snippets of gossip or exchange recipes or opinions on current affairs; on other occasions, they would both remove their armour and completely lay themselves bare, revealing their hopes, fears, dreams or regrets. Their relationship had been reimagined since their days in Kilberry, but it was all the better for it. They were soul mates: they always were and always would be.

Then, one Christmas, a note arrived in place of the traditional greeting card. Granted, Pádraig couldn't hold a candle to the likes of Oscar Wilde or G.B. Shaw in the literary stakes, but as Sister Agatha glanced at the convent's address on the envelope, she became concerned by how illegible her friend's writing had now become. Suspecting that something was amiss, she crept into the empty chapel to read the correspondence in private. As her eyes scanned the opening lines, she felt her throat tighten: Pádraig had cancer, and the prognosis was not promising.

'There's littel to be dun now, xcept to ask for one finel faver.'

Pádraig explained that while he had no fear of death, he regretted his inability to stand up to his despicable mother, particularly when it came to defending his childhood sweetheart and correcting the belief that a farmer's daughter would never amount to anything.

'You have acheeved so much over your life, Butsy, and I could not bee more prowd of you. But, if I may, I wood like to make one small demand before I finelly wither away four good.'

Sister Agatha did not notice the rest of the sisters arriving at the chapel for vespers; she was far too preoccupied reading and re-reading the final lines in the note.

'Prove that old wench wrong and do something so marvelus that your name will bee etched in the history bucks forever. While time isn't on my side, you have plentee of good years a head of you. After all, milk has an expiry date, but life isn't milk.'

Before Sister Agatha could reach the convents front door and make a sprint for the hospital so that she could be by his side, a phone call came with the news that Pádraig had died that afternoon on the Feast of the Immaculate Conception, at the age of seventy-two.

A few days later, as the coffin was lowered into the ground, Sister Agatha clasped the emerald ring in her hand, looked down at her best friend, and repeatedly nodded her head.

'I promise you I will do something sensational,' she whispered. 'I promise I will.'

* * *

Sister Agatha was not immune to grief and struggled severely with her loss. She became irritated by other people's presence; whether they were simply offering her a cup of tea or a friendly smile, she wanted to do like Attila the Hun and gouge their eyes out. (Sister Cecilia rued the day she suggested playing musical chairs following the Christmas turkey...)

Over time, Sister Agatha wisely decided that it might be more advantageous—and law-abiding—to channel her energies into fulfilling the vow she had made to Pádraig instead: to do something so magnificent that universities would be studying her accomplishment for centuries to come. As the years went on and the 'how' of this bold statement remained unclear, Sister Agatha decided to place her faith in God, assured that a plan would emerge one day, which is precisely what happened.

On the morning of her eightieth birthday, everything finally fell into place. Being an octogenarian in a convent was nothing unusual; in fact, you were considered a spring chicken until you passed the century mark. What if, Sister Agatha wondered, she could reach that landmark age and then surpass it by a handful of years and become the oldest person in the world? That would be a feat that would madden the late Mrs Keogh, who didn't even make it to fifty!

From that day forth, she had kept one eye on the prize and the other on her health to ensure that she would accomplish her bold objective. And all was going swimmingly well until a pesky doctor dropped the bombshell of her imminent demise. Ever the chameleon, though, Sister Agatha had adapted to the situation and produced a brave Plan B, which saw her travelling across three continents in under a week before fittingly returning to the village where it all began in 1915.

If Pádraig weren't smiling down upon her now, proud of his old pal's splendid efforts, Sister Agatha would need to get new friends, alive or otherwise, that was for sure!

TWENTY-ONE

'What do you mean you don't know who Riccardo is? He's Pádraig—*your* Pádraig.'

A stunned Ludovico dragged Sister Agatha behind the tree and—for now, at least—away from the world's media. Completely at sixes and sevens, he tried desperately to make sense of what had just been whispered into his ear and prayed that the old gal was simply confused and that her scandalous claims were a manifestation of shock and sorrow. But Sister Agatha showed none of the other traditional symptoms of grief, suggesting that her words might actually be genuine. In ten seconds, the poor chap had aged about forty years.

'I never saw that man once in my life until yesterday,' Sister Agatha repeated, although noticing the abject terror hijacking the nurse's face, she felt she should be a little more sympathetic to his plight—or run the risk of being responsible for his nervous breakdown.

'So, this Pádraig person never existed?'

'He did, of course, and he had the most beautiful blue eyes and the most terrible mother you could imagine, but Pádraig died way back in the late sixties. Although, if he were here today, I know he'd be tickled pink!'

Ludovico could feel an anxiety attack coming on—his breath quickened; his head pounded. Many years had passed since he last suffered such an attack, and following numerous—and expensive—sessions with his therapist, he had hoped that they were well behind him. But under the circumstances, such an intrusion was the least he could expect.

'But you said he was Pádraig!'

'No, I never actually said that,' she calmly replied. 'Although I might have allowed you to believe that they were the same person, I'll admit.'

The nun didn't have much interest in passing any blame; however, if this sweet but incredibly doe-eyed chap wanted to survive in the big, bad world, he desperately needed to hear a bit of tough love.

'Ludovico, when I arrived at Stella della Laguna, it was you and your colleagues who believed that I was some long-lost lover from Riccardo's early life,' Sister Agatha firmly reminded him. 'It was you and your colleagues who thought that I looked like the sculptures in his room. It was you and your colleagues who assumed that the Pádraig in my story—that you and your colleagues demanded I tell—was Riccardo. And it was you and you alone who insisted on bringing him to Ireland. Not me!'

'Oh, Madonna!' Ludovico uttered before collapsing onto his knees.

The courtesy that the media had paid the grieving lover to compose herself in private had now come to an end, and the legion of photographers and camera operators, hungry to get the grieving woman's reaction on camera, emerged from behind the tree.

'But why didn't you say something?' Ludovico pressed. 'You knew that I was mistaken, and you were very much aware that a journey like that would kill him.'

'And as luck would have it, it seems that that is precisely what Riccardo wanted to happen, too,' she reported, leaving the innocent nurse more confused than ever. 'Being a super-centenarian isn't a piece of cake for everyone, you know. Oh, what I'd do for a slice of Black Forest Gateau right now!'

Ludovico jumped to his feet and grabbed her by the arm; their backs now faced the world's media.

'Answer me this then: why did you come to Stella della Laguna in the first place?'

'Because almost fifty years ago, Ludovico, I made an improbable vow to the most important person who ever walked in, and out, and back into my life—and about sixty seconds ago, I realised it, which is why I can't stop smiling.'

'What vow?' he quizzed, his brain valiantly resisting the urge to explode.

'Just before he died, Pádraig asked for my help to settle an old score. He charged me with exacting revenge on his mother, Mrs Keogh, and demanded that I prove her doomed prognosis for me wrong by doing something so marvellous that my name would be etched in the history books forever.'

At that moment, the nurse finally understood everything.

'You decided to become the world's oldest person?'

'Bullseye!' Sister Agatha boldly replied.

'So when you came to Venice, it wasn't to be reunited with Riccardo, but to k—'

'Shhh – nobody likes a tattle-tale, do they?'

She gently took Ludovico's face in her hands, drew it close to her own, and wiped away his tears. 'I have a feeling that this episode will be the making of us both—so long as we keep certain details to ourselves. Understood?'

After planting a kiss on his cheek, sister Agatha returned to her admirers—now that she had been decorated with such a prestigious honour, the oldest person in the world had duties and responsibilities to fulfil, and it just wouldn't do, standing around, yapping all day.

EPILOGUE

THE IRISH INDEPENDENT, 8 FEBRUARY 2026

Today, it seemed as if the rain poured down from the heavens above to make room for its newest arrival, Sister Agatha, who died last Sunday, on what was her 128th birthday, making her the oldest person to have ever lived.

Breaking with the age-old funereal traditions maintained by the Order of Saint Aloysius, Sister Agatha's send-off was a public event—a joyous celebration to say one final farewell to a woman who had become an unlikely romantic heroine in her 13th decade.

Determined to be reunited with her childhood sweetheart, Pádraig Keogh, at the age of 118, Sister Agatha travelled to Venice, where he lived in a residential home for the elderly. With Ludovico Bianchi's assistance, the nun brought him home to Kilberry, County Meath, for one last time. Pádraig died soon after their epic voyage, but only after inspiring the world that nobody is ever too old to have one final adventure.

Taking the mantle of the world's oldest person from her one true love, Sister Agatha then spent the next decade being instrumental in opening a shelter for victims of domestic abuse built on the grounds of the Order of Saint Aloysius' convent in Navan. The centre was primarily funded by an extremely generous donation of over a million euro—made anonymously some ten years ago—and the sale of her stunning emerald engagement ring. The invaluable service has since become a source of envy throughout the world, thanks to its scope, resources and success rate in helping families make fresh starts.

When she wasn't investing her energy into her philanthropic duties, Sister Agatha was a regular fixture on the social scene, frequently appearing on the red carpet for nightclub openings and film premières. One such movie was called *You Don't Know What You've Got Till It's Gondola*, an Oscar-winning biopic of her own story, which Mr Bianchi co-wrote.

Present at the burial included many well-known faces from the celebrity world, not to mention a rainbow of colourful characters who crossed paths with the late nun over the years.

'She transformed my life,' Dougie McGregor, who travelled over from Glasgow for the funeral, said afterwards. 'Thanks to her, I met the love of my life, Tayri Chakchouk, and even though my bride passed away before we cut the wedding cake, those few precious married hours we had together were the most magical of my entire life. Again, it was all thanks to Sister Agatha.'

The 128-year-old's death coincided with the Memorial Day of Saint Agatha of Sicily, the martyred virgin saint whose name she took on entering the convent.

A legend and a champion, Sister Agatha will be deeply missed by all the people she touched throughout her long life. As a parting joke, mourners received much amusement from the quirky epitaph that the super-centenarian requested to be written on her gravestone: '*Milk has an expiry date, but life isn't milk.*'

Amen to that.

ACKNOWLEDGEMENTS

I would like to thank:

My darling agent and friend, Lorraine Brennan, for her unrelenting support and love over the years.

Alexander, for telling me I could write, then allowing me to do so in Irish Tatler Man.

Kemberlee and Peter Shortland at Tírgearr Publishing, who published the first edition of this book in 2016, and my editor, Sharon Pickrel.

The many national tourist offices that hosted me over the years and thus provided me with such excellent material for this novel.

My partner, Gabriele, who bribed me with prosecco and gelato to ensure that I met my daily deadlines. And his parents for welcoming me into their gorgeous home in Venice.

I owe new red pens to the many friends I forced to read early drafts of the manuscript – Vanessa Keogh, Eamonn Norris, Stephen Wall, Gayle Norman and my brother, Déaglán.

And, above all, my parents, who made more sacrifices than any saint in Heaven to afford my siblings and me every opportunity in life. The helicopter pad might still be a pipe dream, but at least I can pay for lunch now!

OTHER BOOKS BY THIS AUTHOR

Colin and the Concubine
Mercier Press

'**Hilarious**' RTE.ie • '**Another winner**' Woman's Way • '**Laugh-out-loud adventure**' Irish Mail on Sunday • '**A natural gift for comedy**' The Gloss

Colin Saint James hates his older brother, Freddie - and for good reason. A true psychopath, Freddie has been hell-bent on destroying Colin's happiness since before he was born! Never one to admit defeat, Colin searches for opportunities to get one up on his sibling, even just once.

When the heats for the final ever Housewife of the Year competition are announced, Colin sees his chance. The only problem is he needs a wife. Luckily, he lives next door to Navan's best-looking woman, Azra, who happens to be single and anxious to get a ring on her finger. But Azra is also a Turkish concubine.

Will Colin be able to park his reservations about his X-rated neighbour if it gives him the chance to emerge triumphant over Freddie for once in his life?

Crazy for You
Mercier Press

'Genuinely hilarious, charmingly intelligent' The Irish Times
• **'Assured, astute and wickedly funny'** Woman's Way • **'Very, very funny'** The Irish Examiner

When Clooney Coyle promises Vonnie Gallagher they'll be friends for life, he has no idea what he's letting himself in for. The lonely and eccentric Vonnie quickly becomes obsessed with the kind-hearted but insecure actor, and her misguided crush soon develops into something much more sinister, leaving Clooney's career in tatters.

But when fate takes a strange turn and elevates the pair into an overnight celebrity couple, Clooney must decide whether to embrace the fame he has longed for since childhood or end the ridiculous charade before Vonnie's jealous - and murderous - inclinations spiral out of control.

MORE ABOUT THIS AUTHOR

Hailing from Navan in the royal county of Meath, Domhnall is a graduate of the Bachelor in Acting Studies Programme, Trinity College Dublin, later completing a Master's in Screenwriting at Dún Laoghaire IADT.

He now works as an actor and a journalist, dividing his time between Galway, where he films TG4's award-winning series, *Ros na Rún*, Dublin and Venice, where he and his Italian lover continuously promise their well-worn livers that they will refrain from quaffing so much prosecco. (Unfortunately, it seems some vows, just like nearby Rome, were not built in a day.)

Wine-drinking aside, for more than four years, Domhnall has also enjoyed the responsibility of being Assistant Editor at *Irish Tatler Man*, a title whose various awards include Consumer Magazine of the Year. Thanks to this role, he interviewed a host of high-profile names such as Tommy Hilfiger, Chris Pine, Kevin Spacey, David Gandy, and Jacques Villeneuve.

Domhnall has written for most of Ireland's leading newspapers and magazines, including the *Irish Independent*, *The Irish Times* and RTE. He also writes a monthly column in *Woman's Way*, the country's biggest-selling weekly magazine.

His first novel, *Sister Agatha: the World's Oldest Serial Killer*, was released in 2016 by Tirgearr Publishing. His second and third books, *Colin and the Concubine* and *Crazy for You*, were published by Mercier Press, Ireland's oldest publishing house.

Printed in Great Britain
by Amazon

41307878R10108